D0228895

'So, *Dr* Roberts, what can I do for you?' The mixed scent of his sweat and cologne instantly invaded her senses, making Missy's head swim with memories of their night together.

'Well, *Sister* Bell, I'm not quite sure,' he said. 'We seem to have got ourselves into a bit of a predicament.'

'You're a distraction,' she said.

'What?'

He flinched backwards and drew his gaze away from hers. She blinked twice. Apparently she was the only person caught in the memory.

'You distracted me at work today, Cooper. It's really difficult to be in a confined space with someone you last saw naked.'

He raised an eyebrow at her candour. 'Get straight to the point, why don't you?'

'It needs to be said.' Her fingers twiddled with a lock of her hair. She was trying to appear cool and casual. 'I felt as if I couldn't concentrate at work today, and that's not me. I'm *very* good at my job.'

Scarlet Wilson wrote her first story aged eight, and has never stopped. Her family have fond memories of *Shirley and the Magic Purse*, with its army of mice, all with names beginning with the letter 'm'. An avid reader, Scarlet started with every Enid Blyton book, moved on to the *Chalet School* series, and many years later found Mills & Boon®.

She trained and worked as a nurse and health visitor, and now currently works in public health. For her, finding Medical™ Romances was a match made in heaven. She is delighted to find herself among authors she has read for many years.

Scarlet lives on the West Coast of Scotland with her fiancé and their two sons.

**This is Scarlet's first book
for Mills & Boon® Medical™ Romance.
Look out for more from her, coming soon!**

IT STARTED WITH A PREGNANCY

BY
SCARLET WILSON

First published in Great Britain 2011
by Mills & Boon, an imprint of Harlequin (UK) Limited.
Large Print edition 2012
Harlequin (UK) Limited, Eton House,
18-24 Paradise Road, Richmond, Surrey TW9 1SR

© Scarlet Wilson 2011

ISBN: 978 0 263 22437 5

LONDON BOROUGH OF
HACKNEY
LIBRARY SERVICES

	OCAT	
ACC. No.	13/008	
CLASS		

IT STARTED WITH A PREGNANCY

For my own three personal heroes: Kevin, Elliott & Rhys.

And to Nancy Holroyd, a valued critique partner, with patience, insight and lots of good advice, and to Rachael Johns for her support and encouragement.

CHAPTER ONE

COOPER noticed her straight away. The music throbbed in his ears as the dozens of bodies around him pushed and jostled to gain a better position at the oak-topped bar. She was standing alone, looking calm and serene, if a little awkward. He knew instantly she wasn't used to being in a place like this. He watched as she sipped at her drink and glanced at her silver watch, her left forefinger twiddling with a strand of chestnut hair. He wished he could reach out and tuck it behind her ear.

'Why don't you go and speak to her?'

The voice made him start. He turned to face his friend Jake, who was pointing in her direction. 'Go on, then. You've been staring at her for the last ten minutes. Go talk to her.'

Cooper frowned. 'Don't be ridiculous. She might be waiting for someone. I can't go and speak to her.' He shook his head in a decided way before picking up his drink again.

Jake put his hand on Cooper's arm. Compassion showed in his dark blue eyes. 'Coop, it's been two years. It's time to get back on the wagon. You're in a new city, with a new job and nobody knows you. Nobody knows your history.'

He gestured in the direction of the beautiful woman. 'Over there is a gorgeous-looking woman, who looks as if some fool has stood her up. This is your chance. Go and take it.' He gave Cooper's arm a little squeeze. 'It's time to start living again.'

Cooper's stomach churned. He felt little beads of sweat breaking out on his forehead. Jake was right. When was the last time he had actually noticed a woman? When was the last time he'd asked a woman out? He couldn't even remember. Last time he could recall his stomach doing flip-flops like this had been at the Christmas dance at school when he'd gone to ask Clara to dance with him. That must have been fifteen years ago.

He glanced over at her again. She was beginning to look uncomfortable. He could take a chance and speak to her or he could go home and sit in his darkened, empty flat—just like he'd done for the last few months. What harm could it do? He took a quick drink from his glass and put it down on the bar. Jake was right. No one knew him here. No one would be looking at him with their sympathetic eyes. No one would describe him as that 'poor consultant who'd been widowed'. No one would talk about the family he'd lost. Here he was just Cooper. It was time for change.

He walked over towards her, but as he neared her his footsteps slowed and his courage started to falter. She turned towards him and their eyes met. Stunning really and they caught him by surprise. Startling bright green. He had expected her eyes to be blue, or brown even, to match her glossy chestnut hair. The emerald-green eyes under long, lustrous eyelashes were bright and clear and for a second he wondered if she was wearing coloured contacts, but then dismissed the idea as he neared her.

The noise in the pub was prohibitive. He would

have to be standing close to her if he wanted to speak to her.

She hadn't moved. Her eyes were still fixed on his. He leaned over to whisper in her ear, his hand automatically resting on her hip. He felt her suck in a breath at his touch. She spoke first, turning her lips towards his ear. 'You've been watching me for the last ten minutes. I wondered when you were going to come and introduce yourself.'

She leaned backwards, a smile dancing across her lips as she noticed the rush of colour in his cheeks. He hesitated for a second, caught off guard as he saw the glint in her eyes. She was teasing him.

He remembered his last thought. It was time for change. He could be a whole new different person. Someone who was confident. Someone who was bold. Someone who believed himself to be attractive and who never went home alone. Tonight, he could be Jake. He cut to the chase. 'Hi, are you waiting for someone?'

She smiled and nodded. 'Yes, my friend appears to have got lost in the ladies.'

He felt a surge of relief—she was here with a

friend. She wasn't waiting for a man. He frowned, his natural instinct taking over. 'Maybe you should go and check on her, she might be unwell.' This time the glint was in his eyes. 'Don't worry, I'll wait for you.'

Her face broke into a wide grin. She raised her eyebrow at him. 'Really?'

She was totally unaware of the captivating picture she made when she smiled. Cooper nodded, gesturing towards the ladies, while the hand that was resting on her hip decided to follow another story and unconsciously pull her closer to him. Her eyes dropped to where his hand was resting. 'Are you planning on letting go of me?'

He pulled his hand back reluctantly and gave a little shrug. 'Sorry'.

She shook her head. 'Actually, I don't think I need to go check on my friend.' She pointed towards the bar. 'She seems to have made her way to another engagement.'

He followed where her finger was pointing and saw a small blonde figure wrapped around a man standing next to the bar.

'Looks like you've been left in the lurch.' He

smiled. He glanced at her empty wine glass. 'So, mysterious woman, can I buy you a drink?'

She glanced at her watch, as if she was weighing up her options. Cooper caught his breath. Don't let her decide to go home! It was only eleven o'clock. She hesitated for a second, before finally handing him her wine glass and fixing him again with her green eyes. 'I'll have a glass of rosé wine, please.'

Cooper took the glass, his fingers brushing hers. He felt the air around him sizzle. This was what it felt like. This was how other people lived. He had forgotten about this side of life. He had forgotten about the feeling in the pit of your stomach when you met someone you were attracted to. He shot her a quick smile and turned towards the bar.

Melissa breathed a huge sigh of relief, the breath hissing out slowly through her tensed lips. She hadn't even realised she'd been holding it. She hadn't believed it when she'd spotted him at the other side of the bar. He was gorgeous. What was he doing in here? Men who looked like that didn't live around here. And what was he doing, talking to her? She took another deep breath, trying to calm the clamouring heart in her chest. She had tried to be blasé when he spoke to her. She had tried to act as if men as handsome as him spoke to her every day. But now she could feel panic setting in. She glanced over at her friend at the bar. Lynn was still wrapped around her latest victim. She would be no help whatsoever.

Cooper turned back around and handed her the wine glass, his fingers brushing hers. She felt the electricity streak up her arm in a delicious buzz. She hadn't been mistaken first time round and she could sense he felt it too. He shot her a beaming smile. 'So, mystery woman, are you going to tell me your name?'

'Melissa,' she replied, before giving a little shake of her head, 'well, Missy.' Her breathing had finally slowed and her heart had stopped hammering on the wall of her chest. She gathered herself and her confidence grew. She could do this. She could talk to the most handsome man for miles. 'My friends call me Missy,' she explained, holding out her hand to shake his.

'Missy,' he repeated, nodding his head as if in

approval. His strong hand caught her slim wrist, giving it a firm shake. And for a few seconds it stayed there, held in an automatic pause because neither party wanted to let go.

'What's yours?'

For a fraction of a second he seemed to hesitate. 'Cooper,' he answered, before regaining his composure and saying, 'Well, actually, my friends call me Coop.'

Her hand reluctantly pulled away from his, her fingers lightly dragging down the palm of his hand, sending delicious shockwaves down his spine. His breath caught in his chest. For a second there he had nearly told her a lie. Just for some wild second he had almost told her his name was Jake. Jake, his friend at the bar, who had no history, no past to haunt him. Jake, who never went home alone. The person he had wanted to be tonight. But he couldn't do it. Not when he was looking into those beautiful eyes. The eyes that were fixed on him right now.

'Pleased to meet you, then, Coop.' She had moved a little closer to him now, the noise in the bar making it difficult to be heard. He caught a waft of her perfume. Not what he'd expected. Something subtle, with a hint of orange. Most women that he knew wore floral scents, but this was something much more scintillating. He inhaled a little deeper, trying to catch her essence.

'What brings you here, Coop?' Her eyes flickered up and down the length of his body. 'I've definitely never seen you around before.'

No. Melissa was absolutely sure she'd never seen him here before. Because he wasn't someone that you'd forget in a hurry. Black shirt tucked into black jeans. Wide shoulders, tapering to a slim waist with long legs and a very watcher-friendly bottom. Then there was his hair. Light brown, slightly longer than normal, which sort of flopped over his right eye. His rich chocolate-coloured eyes. The kind that once you started looking at they drew you in, further and further, until you could almost feel yourself enveloped by the warm hues.

Melissa gave herself a shake. What was she doing? She never had thoughts like this! Even if the man in front of her looked like something from a jeans ad. This was the first time in months she'd felt even vaguely attracted to a man again. Had it really been that long? Had it really been six months since David had stalled once again on starting a family together? Something he knew Melissa desperately wanted. Had it really been six months since Melissa had finally had the courage to call off their engagement? Melissa gave herself another shake. The time span hadn't even registered with her. It was definitely time to move on. Time to move from the lost-in-space zone she'd inhabited for the last six months. And here, right in front of her, was the perfect opportunity.

Cooper gave her a lazy smile, showing off perfect straight white teeth and a little dimple in his right cheek. It made him look like a cheeky schoolboy.

'You're right, I'm not from here. I just moved up this week.'

She quickly glanced at his left hand, cursing herself for not doing it earlier. *Relief, no wedding band.* 'Did you move up yourself?'

Cooper nodded swiftly, taking another quick gulp of his drink. His right hand slipped into his pocket and subconsciously started to touch the cool metal band. He hadn't worn it on his finger for the last few months but he just couldn't bring himself to put it back in the box yet. So he kept it in his pocket, where every now and then he had the urge to reach in and touch it.

'Whereabouts are you staying?'

He nodded towards the right. 'In the new flats, next to the marina. They're only about five minutes from here.'

Melissa felt her stomach flip. She'd seen them. She'd walked through the show flat as if she'd been in a dream world. Or a nightmare, once she'd seen the price. It had been gorgeous, a silver bespoke kitchen with appliances to die for, the most luxurious red velvet sofa she'd ever seen, with cushions you could just sink into, matching curtains with a view over the spectacular marina where all the million-pound boats were moored. And the *pièce de résistance*, the huge white bedroom with mahogany four-poster bed. Every little girl's dream bedroom. The kind of carpet so white you were scared to step on it in case you left a mark. She remembered the blue plastic covers they had been forced to put on over their own shoes before they had been allowed in the show flat. Once she'd seen the white bedroom Melissa had completely understood. He must be a millionaire to own a flat like that.

'So what brings you to Kessington?' she asked curiously. One of the largest towns in the North of England, Kessington had a thriving marina and affluent business district. She wondered what he did for a living. Her interest was definitely piqued.

A frown flickered across his brow. It was the second time she'd seen that moment of hesitation from him. What was he hiding?

His eyes met hers again. Heat flared between them. 'This and that,' he answered dismissively. The noise in the bar swelled again as another crowd of revellers surged through the door. His hand automatically went to her waist again, pulling her closer so that his lips were brushing the top of her earlobe. The movement sent tiny electrical impulses down her spine, leaving the little hairs at the back of her neck standing deliciously on end. Melissa could hear imaginary voices in her head screaming, *He's gorgeous. Go for it, girl!* She could feel her knees start to tremble. When was the last time someone had tried to chat her up? She couldn't even remember. For the first time in her life she felt as if she was about to be swept off her feet, like some damsel in distress being rescued by a white knight on a beautiful stallion. A smile danced across her lips as she stared at the gorgeous man in front of her. If only he could see the picture inside her head right now, he would probably run screaming from the room! She pulled her mind from her fantasy and brought it back to the present. What did 'this and that' mean? Their eyes connected again, leaving her in no doubt that the feelings were entirely mutual.

Cooper gave her a wide smile. This was just what he needed. The last two years at work had been painful. The last year had been especially painful as his colleagues had seemed to decide that the official 'mourning period' should be over. That had resulted in a procession of female colleagues under his nose who had obviously decided he was an eligible bachelor again. It had become almost painful to have a conversation with a member of the female staff. It hadn't helped that hospitals seemed to have an unending supply of women. Heavy hints had been dropped all around him, telling him it was time to move on.

But this was different. This was his decision. To see a beautiful woman in a bar and have a conversation with her. To know that he felt attracted to her. There was freedom in this that he'd never experienced before and it felt like a huge weight had been lifted off his shoulders. He didn't even want to think about work right now. He gave a little sigh. His eyes swept downwards. The thin fabric of her green dress clung to her curves, showing just enough of her cleavage to give him a hint of what lay beneath. He found his voice again. 'What about you?'

Melissa was conscious of his fingers at her waist. Tingles swept along her skin where his hand lay, causing her to suck her breath in again deeply. There was something enticing about the mystery between them. She liked the fact that someone, especially a tall, dark handsome someone, was interested in her. She decided to play him at his own game.

She threw back her head, tossing her chestnut curls over her shoulder. 'I'm a bit like yourself,' she teased, a twinkle in her eyes, 'a bit of this and a bit of that.'

Cooper almost laughed. He could see the flicker of panic that whizzed across her face. He knew she wasn't used to this. But then again, neither was he. He hadn't felt this good in a long time. It made him determined not to let this night end. He leaned forward, his breath on the skin at the side of her neck. 'So, mysterious Missy, let's have some fun.'

She delighted in the shivers that quivered down her spine and the thoughts that were immediately conjured up in her mind. His voice was rich and husky; it made him all the more attractive to her. *Boy, he was sexy.*

Her bright eyes fixed on his. 'What do you mean?' Was it time for her to start panicking? How had he interpreted what she'd just said? This was so unlike her. She wasn't used to meeting men in pubs and having flirtatious conversations.

But there was just something about him that was irresistible. And she knew she didn't want this to end.

'Well, I don't know much about you—you don't know much about me. How about we remedy that?' His hand around her waist had tightened its grip, turning her around to face him. Her breasts were now skimming his chest. She could feel the response of her nipples underneath the confines of her clingy dress. On an ordinary day she would have been horrified and embarrassed, but tonight she didn't even look down—she didn't have to—she just moved a little closer.

His right hand came out from his pocket to rest on her other hip. 'I've got a suggestion. Some questions—but only completely truthful answers.' His smile was a little crooked, so he wasn't quite so perfect after all.

She raised herself up on her tiptoes, her hands resting on his broad shoulders as she whispered in his ear, 'I think I'm up for that.'

He looked quickly round the crowded bar. 'It's too noisy in here. Let's take a walk,' he said, turning her towards the door. He lifted her thick black coat and held it open for her to slip her arms inside. Melissa glanced around the bar. She couldn't see her friend at the bar any more and didn't want to waste time looking for her. She'd probably already left without her. Her stomach fluttered a little. She didn't do this. She didn't meet strange men in pubs and leave with them. She was Melissa. Reliable. Dependable. Great in a crisis. Sister in the labour ward and the most sensible person that even she knew. No one would believe her if she told them about this. Part of that was the attraction. Missy instinctively felt safe with him and her instincts had always been good. She'd spent the last six months eating, sleeping and working. There was more to life and she knew it. It was time to throw caution to the wind and act on instinct. And it felt delicious.

His hand pressed gently on her back as he ushered her through the crowd and out the door. The biting cold wind hit her immediately and she fastened her coat up round her neck. He stood next to her, patiently waiting. 'Give me a second,' she said, pulling her mobile from her pocket. 'I'm just going to send my friend a text to let her know

I've left.' She dabbed quickly on the keypad, her fingers rapidly going white with cold, before finally pressing 'Send'. She lifted her hands to her mouth, blowing on them to try and revive them. In an instant she felt his warm hand encircle hers and she stuck the other hand deep in her pocket, pushing her phone away safely. A smile danced across her face as she pictured her friend receiving the text

Left with the gorgeous man in black WOO HOO!

Lynn would be stunned. She hadn't met the new, reckless Melissa. She was used to the sensible friend who made sure she got home safely at the end of the night. Another little wave of excitement ran through Melissa. *This felt good.*

'Let's go this way,' Cooper said as he automatically turned towards the marina. She felt her heart quicken in her chest. The roads and pavements were glistening with frost that was starting to form on the cold winter's night. She grasped his hand a little tighter. Her beautiful black high-heeled shoes were a joy to look at, but not so much of a joy to walk in. She teetered along precariously next to him, shooting him a smile and pretending to walk with confidence.

'So, Missy,' he said, 'tell me a bit about yourself. Do you often leave pubs with strange men?'

'Oh.' She was caught off guard. She stopped walking abruptly. 'Of course I don't!' The words came out more harshly than she'd expected. Did he think she was easy?

'Calm down,' he said quietly, moving his arm around her waist. 'It's all right, Missy. I kind of guessed this was all new to you.'

'You did?' Her wide eyes met his steady gaze. His deep eyes pulling her in even closer.

'Yes, I did,' he said assuredly. 'Would it help if I told you I was new at all this too?'

'You are?' She could hardly believe it. Surely women were beating down his door with a stick?

He gave her a nod, pulling her a little closer. 'Now relax. You're safe with me. Tell me something unusual. What's the one thing most people don't know about you? Something that only your good friends would know.'

Her mind was spinning and her heart was beating frantically in her chest again. How did this man do this to her? How could one man cause her body to be all aquiver and turn her brain to mush? She'd expected him to ask her something mundane. Her befuddled brain blurted out the first answer that came into her head. 'I'm a sci-fi freak.'

'Wow!' He stopped walking and turned to look at her under the yellow streetlight. Nothing could change the glow coming from those beguiling green eyes. He couldn't hide the amusement on his face. 'Really? Well, you've certainly surprised me.'

'Why?' She tried to look offended, before adding defensively, 'I think they're the most exciting films in the cinema. Give me anything with a laser gun and spacesuit and I'm sold. Take me to see a chick flick and you've had it.'

'Mmm.' He looked her up and down.

'What?'

'I'm just imagining you in one of those *really* short space dresses.' He nodded approvingly. 'I'm liking what I see.'

'Get lost!' She thumped him through his thick grey jacket. 'Right, my turn. Are you the chick-flick type?'

She waited for his answer while silently scolding herself. She needed to get some more imagination if she wanted to win this game.

'Westerns,' he said decisively. 'All that testosterone, horses and guns blazing. Any boy's dream.'

A testosterone-loving man. She wondered how much she should read into that. 'My turn this time.' As they came to an icy puddle on the pavement, he wrapped his arm further around her waist and pulled her towards his hip.

She felt oddly comfortable tucked under his protective hold. She lifted her head as she heard some people pass by on the other side of the street. From over there they would look like a couple in love, wrapped around each other on a cold winter's night. A couple of young women walked around them on the pavement, both women's eyes automatically running up and down Cooper's body with unhidden admiration. Melissa smiled. *Look all you want, ladies, this man is with me.* From this position she raised her head, her nose brushing against his cold cheek, and looked straight into his magnetic eyes. The smallest of gestures. The most intimate of gestures. She wanted this night to last forever. Her brain pulled itself into focus. It was time for another question. 'What do you like to read?'

He nodded in recognition of the question, taking a few seconds to decide on his answer. He let out a big sigh. 'Is this the point I'm supposed to tell you I don't read much? Because I fear I'm about to reveal a childhood secret.'

Her face lit up with a bright smile. 'Then I think I will too, so go ahead.'

'I love to read. I always have done. So it's absolutely got to be any of the old-fashioned detective novels. But I mean really old, long before everything became so scientific and crimes were solved with DNA and microscopic evidence. I always loved them as a child. Even now as an adult I still sometimes pick them up. I love the characters.'

She gave him a curious smile. 'Okay, now I'm intrigued. What's so good about the characters?'

'Everything. Their intelligence. Their wit. Even their complications. Sometimes even their mistakes. I loved them all.' She was staring at him again with those luminescent eyes. Her chestnut curls were waving gently in the wind. It was all he could do not to reach up and run his fingers through her tresses. Then his hand would be at the back of her head and he could pull her towards him…

Her face was shining. 'For me it was the classics, particularly *Little Women*, which I still read on occasion. The copy I have is so tatty and dog-eared that some of the pages are about to fall out. I still cry every time I read it. It breaks my heart when Beth dies.'

He watched. She was so caught up in what she was saying her eyes were glistening with unshed tears. Something tugged at his heartstrings. Something almost primal. When was the last time he'd felt this protective towards a woman?

She caught the expression on his face and it stopped her as she was about to continue. She sensed the deep emotions that were smouldering inside him. But what were they? Was it a memory? Or was it something more primitive, like lust?

They'd reached the marina and were now standing next to the barrier, looking out over the array of million-pound boats, all costing more than Melissa would earn in a lifetime. His arm was still locked firmly around her waist.

His voice cut through the darkness. 'Let's go with the dream theme. What would be your dream job?'

Instantly her voice caught in her throat. Missy had her dream job. Being a midwife was the only job she had ever wanted to do, and would ever want to do. But for some reason she wasn't inclined to tell him that. He'd been coy about work earlier. He didn't want to talk about it. So she intended to be coy too.

It was easier to stick with the sci-fi theme. 'My dream job would be an astronaut.' She waved her arm above her head. 'To fly amongst the stars would be magical.'

'And the reason you didn't train at NASA?' he queried playfully.

She heaved a huge sigh and turned, releasing

herself from his grasp and leaning backwards against the railings. 'What can I say? I failed physics at school and I think it was a basic requirement of astronaut training. So that put me out.'

'What a shame,' Coop said, standing directly in front of her and putting a hand on either side of her hips. He pulled her gently towards him. 'I could have met you there.' He lowered his face towards hers, his breath visible in the cold night air.

'You're telling me that was your dream job too?' she whispered. Her face was only inches from his.

'Absolutely. Just look at how much we have in common. We were obviously destined to meet.' He ran his hands around her hips, cradling her bottom. She caught her breath at the intimacy of the movement. A word sang in her head. Destiny. She knew it was crazy but it certainly felt like that. What if somewhere, in some lifetime, this gorgeous man was indeed her perfect match? What if she hadn't spoken to him? What if she'd gone home early? What if she'd been too scared to throw caution to the wind and leave with him—something she would never normally have done?

But everything about this felt perfect. She felt as if she was meant to be there, in his arms, at this moment. Everything about this just felt so right.

He gave her a slow smile. 'See,' he whispered, 'we're a match made in heaven.' She moved closer, her hips pressing against his, her hands resting on his shoulders. She shivered. 'It's really cold out here.' Her eyes met his.

'We could go inside.' His lips brushed against her ear. 'You might have failed physics at school but how did you do at biology?'

Melissa's heart stopped. 'I got first prize,' she said breathlessly.

The words hung in the darkness for a few seconds. Both knew where this was leading. Melissa could feel the heat between their bodies. She knew she should say no. She knew she should walk away. But she didn't want to. She hardly knew anything about Coop. She didn't even know his second name. But, then, he didn't know hers.

Most of all, she didn't want to walk away. She wanted to have this one night of reckless passion with this mysterious stranger. She wanted to break free from the 'sensible' sign that followed her wherever she went. She wanted to follow her destiny. After all, who would ever know? She dropped her hand from his shoulder and placed her hand in his.

He led her wordlessly to the front door of the flats she had viewed earlier that year. They entered the lift and she stifled a gasp when he pressed the button for the top floor. Moments later he opened his front door into the flat of her dreams.

'You bought the show flat?' she asked in astonishment.

He nodded nonchalantly. 'It seemed easier just to buy the one with the furniture included.' He spread his arms out around the wide space. 'I was never any good at that sort of thing anyway.'

He gestured towards her and she handed him her thick coat, which he hung in a nearby cupboard. Melissa walked in awe around the open-plan kitchen, running her finger along the black marble worktop, her heels clicking on the slate floor. Cooper turned and opened the blinds in the living area to show the view over the marina. If she'd thought it was stunning downstairs, up here it was breathtaking. The boats glistened, gleaming white against the black water. Her fingers automatically went up to touch the red curtains. They were thick and luxurious, just as she'd imagined. She pointed towards the sumptuous sofa that she'd admired from afar. 'Can I?'

Coop looked puzzled. 'Of course.'

She sank into the huge cushions, closed her eyes and let out a huge sigh. 'Oh, it's just as gorgeous as I imagined.' She snuggled her shoulders deeper into the soft fabric.

'What are you talking about?'

Her eyes flickered open. 'I came to see this flat when it was the show flat for the development and I *really, really* wanted to do this.'

'You wanted to sit on the sofa?' His right eyebrow rose in amusement.

'Well—yes, but the woman that was showing us around was a bear and I was too scared to touch anything. I think she could tell just by looking that I could never afford to stay anywhere like this.'

Cooper let out a laugh. It was deep, warm and rich. Not what she had expected.

Her train of thought hadn't shifted. 'So how can you afford this?'

He lowered his eyes slightly. 'I came into some money and I earn a relatively good salary.' He plumped down next to her on the oversized sofa.

Melissa nodded. She could tell when not to press him. She turned sideways to face him. 'Whose turn is it to ask a question?'

He ran his finger down her arm, causing her skin to come out in tiny goose-bumps. 'I've lost track,' he whispered, leaning forward and twisting a finger in her chestnut curls, pulling her face towards his.

She expected his kiss to be light, gentle, and it was anything but. It was hard and passionate, instantly setting her body alight with desire. She felt the heat spreading throughout her being. Heat she hadn't felt in months—no, heat like this she had never felt. His other hand came up and caught the other side of her head, cradling her face. He drew his head back from hers, looking her in the eye. 'I didn't have any plans like this tonight,' he said sincerely, 'but right now I'm going to ask you if you want to come through to the bedroom with me.'

Melissa went to speak but he placed one finger on her lips. 'Shh. Missy, if you want to leave I won't stand in your way. But I would really like it if you'd stay.' His breath was slightly ragged now, as if he was trying to fight the fire building inside him.

Her heart was pounding. This was sexual chemistry like she'd never felt before. She reached her hands around his neck and whispered in his ear.

His eyes lit up with wild excitement. 'What was that?' he asked in amazement.

'My next question,' Melissa said with quiet assurance. 'I just decided what I wanted to ask.'

Cooper looked at her with his steady brown eyes, a smile forming across his lips. 'In that case, this takes me back to show and tell from school, and this answer is definitely a show.' And he took her by the hand and led her to the white bedroom.

CHAPTER TWO

Eight weeks later

MELISSA had just finished zipping up her tunic when she heard the shouting at the top of the labour ward. Hurrying to pull her newly washed curls back into a ponytail, she straightened her tunic, and set off down the corridor at speed.

Melissa had been one of the sisters in the labour ward for nearly three years and when she was on duty she prided herself on the calm running of the ward. Today, though, the midwives station at the central point in the labour ward seemed to be in chaos. Melissa tried to make herself heard above the rabble surrounding her. Two junior doctors appeared to be having an argument, two midwives were trying to deal with telephone calls, one consultant was angrily trying to attract the attention of anyone at all, and in the midst of it all stood a man, holding an empty jug of water.

He was holding it out gingerly, saying, 'Excuse me, excuse me?'

Melissa shook her head, lengthening her last few strides as she reached the station. 'Enough!' Her hand thudded on the desk and immediately silenced her bickering colleagues. 'You two...' she pointed at the junior doctors '...take your discussion elsewhere. My midwives are trying to deal with telephone enquiries.' She grabbed one of the passing nursing auxiliaries, 'Fran, can you assist this gentleman, please?' she asked, gesturing in the direction of the bewildered man.

Finally she turned to the consultant standing at the desk. 'Dr Mackay, can I help you with something?'

He nodded and pointed towards the nearby room. 'I need a set of notes for the lady in Room 4, Katherine Kelly. I'm not happy with her presentation.'

Melissa nodded and walked around to the other side of the midwives' station and retrieved a set of case notes from the trolley. It was the same place where notes had been kept on the labour ward for the last twenty years. She handed him the buff-coloured folder. He took them with a sigh of relief, 'Thank God you're on duty today,' he muttered as he turned and headed back down the corridor.

Melissa watched his retreating back with a smile on her face. Had that been a compliment? Dr Mackay was not famed for his compliments. He was nearing retirement and becoming increasingly grumpy with age. A new consultant had been appointed but Melissa hadn't met him yet.

She waited until one of the midwives at the desk had hung up her phone. 'Carrie, what's going on in here today?'

'Just what you'd expect. The new junior and senior doctors have started today and the place is in chaos. We seem to have more women in labour than usual and we've had a few late presentations with complications.' She pointed in the direction of the midwifery suite. 'Sister Baird is in charge of the midwifery side today—she can update you on the admissions. Jen Connell was in charge of the medical side—she's still in Room 4 with the patient Dr Mackay just collected the notes for.'

Melissa nodded and set off towards the midwifery unit to touch base with her colleague. The labour ward was divided into two sides: the midwifery side, where women with routine pregnancies and routine labours were looked after by a team of midwives from start to finish; and the medical side, where women with high-risk pregnancies were looked after by a team of doctors and midwives. Both sides of the labour ward had a midwifery sister or senior midwife on duty at all times, along with a team of more junior midwives to help support all women through the labour process. Melissa had always worked on the medical side. She had been diabetic since childhood and in this hospital all women with diabetes were automatically under the care of the medical staff. Knowing how single-minded the medical staff could be made Melissa all the more determined that women like her had the best possible birth experience. The only way that would happen was if experienced midwives like her worked hand in hand with their medical associates.

She heard her colleague's voice and pushed

open the nearest door. 'Hi, Andrea.' Her colleague looked up from the foetal monitor she was watching. 'Just letting you know that I'll be taking over in the medical side. Let me know if there are any patients you need to discuss.'

Andrea tucked a stray piece of short blonde hair behind her ear and shot her a quick smile as she pressed a button on the monitor for a printout of the foetal heart. 'Any word on our lady with the breech presentation yet?'

Melissa shook her head. 'I haven't had a report yet from Jen—I'm just going to see her. It was bedlam at the midwifery station when I arrived.'

Andrea gave her a big smile. 'So you haven't seen the new consultant yet? I believe he's in with that patient. She arrived less than an hour ago, already in labour with a breech presentation. We had to transfer her over to the medical side.'

She crossed the room away from the patient she was dealing with and whispered under her breath, 'He's spent the last month covering all the outlying areas, but he's here permanently now. Hunk, total hunk.'

'What?'

'You'll see. Let me know how the patient does, will you?'

Melissa gave her a quick nod and ducked back out of the door. The three midwives she would be working with were waiting at the midwives' station and she assigned them each to an area of the ward before going to take over from Jen.

'Hi, Jen,' she said breezily as she entered the room, crossing behind the curtains to join Jen and the patient. 'I'm here to take over from you—can you give me a report?'

Jen looked up from the notes she had just finished writing and put her pen down. 'Hi, Missy, that's great. Thanks.'

The woman lying on the bed was pale and sweating. Her dark hair lay limp in a cloud around her white face. She was breathing shallowly, small rapid gasps, leaning forward at first and then sagging back against the pillows whenever another contraction took hold. As an experienced midwife Melissa could tell from the shape of the woman's abdomen that the baby was in the wrong position.

Jen continued quickly, 'This is Katherine Kelly.

She's twenty-two and this is her first pregnancy. She missed her last two antenatal appointments and presented in labour just under an hour ago. Her contractions were only four minutes apart when she arrived and it was noticed on admission that baby was in the frank breech position. Her blood pressure had also spiked so she was transferred through to the medical side.' She handed the observation chart she was holding over to Melissa, who cast her eyes over it rapidly.

'She's 40 weeks' gestation. We've just done an ultrasound to confirm the position and size of the baby. Everything looks normal. Her contractions are now two minutes apart. We are too late to turn the baby, and Dr Mackay had been considering Caesarean section, but thankfully our new consultant...' she gestured into the corner of the room '...has plenty of experience of this type of delivery and is happy to take the lead.'

Melissa nodded, assimilating all the information she'd just been given. If Katherine had attended her last two antenatal appointments it was likely that the breech presentation would have been picked up beforehand and dealt with.

Now it meant that the baby was going to come out bottom first instead of head first. Some congenital malformations could result in a breech presentation but the ultrasound must have ruled that out. This meant that all that was really left to do now was to assist the new consultant in the delivery of this baby.

She sat on the bed next to Katherine and took her hand. 'Hi,' she said, 'I'm Melissa and very soon I'm going to help you have this baby.' She turned to face Jen again. 'Is the paediatrician on his way?'

Jen nodded. 'He said he'd be here in the next five minutes.'

Melissa fastened the blood-pressure cuff around Katherine's arm and set the machine to record every five minutes. She turned to face the new consultant in the corner of the room and stretched out her hand towards him. 'Pleased to meet you. I'm Melissa Bell, one of the midwifery sisters.'

He looked up from the notes he had been checking over and her heart froze. Time stopped. Cooper. *Cooper was the new consultant obstetrician?*

Cooper—the man who'd said he did a bit of 'this and that'. Cooper, the man who lived in the show flat overlooking the marina. Cooper, the man who had taken her through to the glistening white bedroom with the mahogany four-poster bed and…

Cooper ran one of his hands through his floppy brown hair and reached his other hand out to meet hers. 'Pleased to meet you, Melissa. I'm Cooper Roberts.' Not a flicker of recognition. His actions were as smooth as silk, the consummate professional.

He stood up from his chair and pushed the bed table he had been leaning on away from him. Melissa hadn't moved. She stood rooted to the spot. The last time she'd seen this man they'd both been naked and he'd been trailing his tongue around every part of her body, awakening sensations she'd never felt before. Her brain was spinning so fast that she thought she might fall over. She wrenched her hand free of his, conscious of the electricity that had just shot up her arm, and grasped the bottom of the bed. Cooper moved effortlessly past her and sat down on the side of the bed to talk to Katherine.

'Is there anyone with you?'

Katherine shook her pale head. 'No, it's just me. My mum lives miles away. I phoned her early this morning but I don't think she'll be here in time.'

'Is there anyone else I can phone for you?'

Melissa was still in shock. She knew what he was doing and why he was doing it. A breech delivery could be traumatic and it would be better if Katherine had someone to support her. He spoke soft, reassuring words to Katherine, whilst resting his hand on her abdomen and explaining how the delivery would proceed.

'If my baby is the wrong position, shouldn't I have a Caesarean section?'

Cooper glanced at her chart. 'From your history you've been in labour for more than twenty-four hours. Your waters have broken and we've already examined you and established that you're fully dilated.' He held her hand reassuringly. 'If we'd known about the baby's position in advance we may well have considered a Caesarean section. But you're pretty far along now and the baby is ready to come out. There's no reason to think there will be any problems.' He gave her hand a little squeeze as another contraction clearly gripped her. 'Do you feel the sensation to push yet?'

Katherine's face crumpled and she nodded. She was clearly growing tired. 'I just want this to be over.' She started to sob.

The blood-pressure cuff round her arm automatically started to inflate again and Cooper's eyes followed the reading carefully. The door opened and the paediatrician appeared, pushing a special cot to allow assessment of the newborn. He gave Cooper a quick nod. 'Nice to see you again, Dr Roberts.' Then shot a smile over towards her. 'And you, Melissa.'

Melissa started. What was she doing? She had to get hold of herself. Cooper had managed to keep his composure without any problems. But it was claustrophobic being in a room with a man she'd seen naked. Naked. There was that word again. She couldn't get it out of her head. But if she closed her eyes for a second she could see his broad torso and muscular arms, all with a little smattering of dark hair that curled downwards towards…

'Sister Bell… Missy?'

She spun abruptly, caught by the informal use of her name. That was what she'd told him to call her that night. His dark chocolate eyes were watching her carefully. He was cool and composed. His gaze never faltered. The ultimate professional. He expected her to be the same.

'Are you ready to assist me?'

Melissa gave a quick nod, tearing her eyes away from his. She moved swiftly over the bed to help assist Katherine into the most appropriate position for delivery at the end of the bed. The semi-recumbent position would allow space at the end of the bed for the baby to hang. Cooper washed his hands and pulled on some gloves before positioning himself at the end of the bed, while Melissa remained at Katherine's side, monitoring the recordings from the foetal monitor and blood-pressure gauge. Cooper swiftly examined Katherine again.

'Okay, Katherine. The baby's bottom is right at the cervix. On your next contraction you can start to push. We'll let you know if you need to stop. Just let us know how you're feeling.'

Katherine nodded tensely as the next contraction took hold of her body. Cooper continued to talk to her quietly but firmly over the next few minutes. 'Good, Katherine, keep pushing. That's the posterior buttock, now the anterior buttock.' The baby's legs were spontaneously delivered. He nodded swiftly at Melissa and the paediatrician to let them know that things were proceeding smoothly. 'Take a deep breath again, Katherine. Things are going well.'

Melissa watched carefully as Cooper delivered the baby's shoulders then checked the position of the arms and umbilicus. If the baby's arms were extended, that could cause problems with the delivery.

'Get ready, people, the baby's arms are flexed so they'll be delivered on the next push.' He shot Katherine a big smile. He had managed to put the patient at ease and was clearly confident in his clinical abilities. 'We're nearly there now, Katherine, just another few big pushes.'

Katherine grimaced and gathered herself for

the next push, gripping Melissa's hand so tightly that she thought her bones might break. Melissa sat down on the bed, wrapping her arm around Katherine's shoulders. 'Do you know what you're having?' she asked, trying to distract her into letting go of her other hand.

Katherine shook her head fiercely. 'I didn't want to know. I wanted a surprise.'

Melissa nodded in understanding. Her view of the earlier ultrasound had revealed the baby's sex but she wasn't about to let Katherine know. She felt Katherine's abdominal muscles begin to tense again. 'Another big push now.'

Cooper positioned his hand to check the position of the baby's head. 'Okay, it's going to be the Burns-Marshall manoeuvre,' he said, clarifying the position to the waiting team. 'This might be a little uncomfortable, Katherine, as we need to turn the baby one hundred and eighty degrees and we have to do it slowly to prevent sudden changes in pressure.'

With his focus entirely on the job in hand, Cooper grasped the baby's ankles, waited for the hairline to appear and then slowly pivoted the baby until the nose and mouth were free. There was silence in the room for the two minutes while he carried out the procedure and the staff silently held their breath. When it was done Cooper handed the baby over to the waiting arms of the paediatrician, who made a quick assessment and used some suction to clear the baby's airways. A quick whiff of oxygen later and the room was filled with the angry roar of a baby who was well and truly awake. The paediatrician gave Melissa a little nod and she picked up a nearby blanket to wrap round the screaming bundle, who was rapidly turning a nice shade of pink.

Just for a second she stopped. This was one of the moments that she loved. Those first few minutes where the baby adjusted to its new surroundings. Some hated the transition and screamed, others were mesmerised and looked around wildly with unfocused eyes. Those first few seconds were precious and it was one of the reasons Melissa loved her job so much. Her stomach gave a little squeeze as she stared at the little one in her arms. When would it be her turn? Would she ever be the person whose heart filled with joy at the first sight of her baby? Her biological clock was ticking and with no potential partner on the horizon, a baby was a long way off.

She glanced down once more at the perfect little pink face in her arms and pulled her mind back into the present.

'Here we go, Katherine,' she said, handing over the precious gift. 'Meet your son.'

Katherine seemed oblivious to the noise in the room and took him with trembling arms. 'Isn't he gorgeous?' she breathed heavily.

Melissa sat down next to her on the bed. 'Have you got a name picked out for him yet?'

Katherine nodded. 'I'm going to name him James, after my dad.'

'That's lovely. I'm sure he'll be delighted.'

She looked up as one of the junior midwives stuck her head around the door. 'Just to let you know that Katherine's mum has arrived.' She caught sight of the little bundle lying Katherine's arms. 'Oh, great, the baby is here. Do you want me to send her in?'

Melissa turned to Katherine. 'We're not quite

finished yet, but do you want her to come in and see the baby?'

Katherine nodded silently. Her eyes hadn't left her baby's. She was still in the newborn glow of motherhood.

Melissa looked at Cooper carefully. It had been her first experience of the new consultant and it was one of the smoothest breech deliveries she had ever seen. He clearly knew his stuff. Melissa went to leave the room and find Katherine's mother. She brushed past Cooper, who was standing talking quietly to the paediatrician. It was a tight squeeze and her breasts brushed against the back of Cooper's white coat. 'Sorry,' she muttered on the way past, and breathed a sigh of relief as she ducked out of the door.

Cooper finished his conversation with the paediatrician and had a few final words with Katherine before picking up her notes and carrying them out the room.

His registrar was waiting outside the room for him. 'Anything I can do, Cooper?'

He nodded quickly. 'Yes. Katherine still has to

deliver her placenta. Can you go and supervise for me?'

Cooper didn't normally like to leave a patient immediately after delivery but he was still getting over the shock of seeing Melissa in the room. He walked into the nearest consulting room and closed the door behind him. Sitting at the desk, his hand automatically went to his trouser pocket where he turned his wedding ring over and over in his pocket.

What on earth was she doing here? He'd been dumbfounded when she'd walked into the room. She hadn't even noticed him to begin with, she'd been too focused on the patient. But when she had seen him she'd looked as if she'd been hit with a ton of bricks. It was obvious she hadn't wanted to see him again. He'd realised that as soon as he'd woken up the next morning and she'd gone. No note. No nothing. Wham! Bam! Thank you, Ma'am!

She hadn't seemed like that type of girl. He'd almost believed she'd never had a one-night stand before. But six weeks later and with no sign of her, his opinion had changed. The last place he'd expected to see her was on the first day of his new job. Why hadn't she told him she was a midwife? He groaned and put his head in his hands. But he hadn't told her he was a doctor either. She had been stunned to see him.

He'd come here to be a new person. He'd wanted to be in a new place where no one knew his history. He wanted to be in a place where he had no ties. Where he could just focus on the job. This was a nightmare. Once word got out he'd slept with the ward sister he would be at the mercy of the hospital grapevine. It had been bad enough at his old post, where everyone had seemed to have a 'wonderful single female friend who would be just perfect for him.' He didn't want to mix business with pleasure. He hadn't even really decided if he was ready for the pleasure side. Cooper sighed and leaned back in his chair. This was the last thing that he wanted. He'd had experience of the hospital grapevine. The whispered words *'That's the consultant whose wife died'* had haunted him for months. That was why he was here. In a new place where there would be no discussion about his personal life, no interference. And now this.

He couldn't bear it. This was the job he loved. This was the one constant in his life. This was the thing that still gave him a reason to get up in the morning, because even after everything that had happened to him, this was the job he was good at. There were patients who needed him, patients that he *could* save. Other doctors might have hidden away, retrained and entered a different branch of medicine, but that had never even entered his mind. His own hospital had held too many painful memories to stay, but here it was different—here a whole new set of memories was waiting to be made and he couldn't allow anything to spoil that for him. He had to be the ultimate professional. This was work and he could manage to maintain a professional relationship with Sister Bell. Couldn't he?

Sister Bell—that was exactly how he would think of her. Not Melissa and certainly not Missy. No. He stood up and straightened his white coat. He could do this.

* * *

Cooper's eyes scanned over the sports arena. He'd been too late to catch Melissa at work but one of the other midwives—Andrea, after wrinkling her nose at him—had told him that she usually came for a run after work. He spotted the figure at the other side of the running track. He'd recognise that body anywhere and that thought triggered a little twist in his gut.

Just as she'd caught his eye in the pub, so she caught his eye here too. She was wearing a bright red tracksuit with a grey running vest and white trainers. Her chestnut hair was pulled up in a ponytail and he watched as she finished her lap and checked the time on her watch. He started to jog slowly around the track towards her. He didn't even know what he was going to say. That he was sorry? That this was awkward? That every time he saw her he had flashbacks to their night together?

He watched as she sat down on the arena steps and pulled her rucksack towards her, pulling a mini chocolate bar from it and eating it in two bites. Then she leaned forward and rested her head on her arms, obviously trying to catch her breath. He slowed as he approached her; there was no time like the present.

Melissa's heart was pounding. She checked her pulse then wondered if her heart was pounding due to her exercise or the day she'd just had at work. The events of the day played over and over in her mind like some bad Groundhog day.

She felt her cheeks flush as she remembered when she'd had to brush past him. Just as well she'd been wearing a hideous sports bra under her uniform. She would have died if he'd noticed her nipples' automatic response. She wasn't used to being haunted by erotic thoughts at work. Which seemed strange since she used to work with her ex, David. But David hadn't conjured up the wild responses that she'd experienced with Cooper. If this was what happened to her mind after one day, how on earth was she going to work with him?

Then there was the fact he hadn't told her he was a doctor—worse, an obstetrician. She'd just come out of a relationship with a doctor and she certainly wasn't looking for another! Why on earth did he have to be working here?

She groaned and stuck her head in her hands. Oh, wake up, Missy! She'd met him in a pub that was five minutes away from the hospital—a known haunt of hospital personnel. He'd picked a flat that was less than a ten-minute walk from the hospital. Most of the new staff tended to look for properties close by, until they had a chance to get to know the local area. And he'd been a new face, someone she'd never seen before. She should have known he was a doctor.

Junior doctors changed jobs every six months, some seniors did too, registrars usually every couple of years, but always around the same time of year. But he was a consultant. Come to think of it, he was pretty young to be a consultant obstetrician. But then again, what age was he?

She couldn't remember if she'd asked him that—she was sure she hadn't. And there weren't many details about that night she'd forgotten. No, she'd spent the last six weeks reliving that night over and over in her head.

How could she work with this man? The

thought of seeing him every day sent delicious tingles along her spine. He was one of the most handsome men she'd ever seen. She'd seen him under cover of darkness before and through a haze of wine, and sometimes that hid a multitude of sins. But not for Cooper. No, he was just as much a Greek god in the cold, harsh light of day as he'd been on that crisp winter's night. She knew that already he'd be the talk of the hospital. There weren't that many handsome, unattached doctors in their midst. She could probably write a list of the names of colleagues who would attempt to ensnare him. That gave her a little flare of, what—jealousy? About someone she hardly knew?

She remembered the delicious excitement that night of leaving with the mysterious stranger. She remembered her thoughts about destiny. She remembered her thought, *Who would ever know?* Melissa groaned. Once. Just once in her life she'd thrown caution to the wind and acted on her instincts. Everything about that night had been magical. So much so that when she'd woken in the morning she'd picked up her clothes and crept out, reluctant to do anything to break the spell from the night before. But at work she was sensible Melissa. Reliable, dependable and good at her job, not the bumbling, distracted idiot she'd felt like today. She wanted to keep her personal and professional lives separate. She was going to have to speak to him. There really wasn't any way around this.

She lifted her head at the slowing footsteps approaching her. Missy was startled. He was the absolute *last* person she expected to see right now.

He slowed his jog and walked the last couple of steps towards her in his navy jogging shorts and T-shirt. No other clothes could showcase his muscled legs so perfectly. A wicked thought filled her mind and instantly a smile danced across her lips as he thumped down next to her.

She leaned back against the steps. 'So, *Dr* Roberts, what can I do for you?' The mixed scent of his sweat and cologne instantly invaded her senses, making her head swim with memories of their night together.

That was it. That was what he'd loved about

her. That had been the attraction—the fact she wasn't afraid to say whatever was on her sassy mind. He leaned back against the steps next to her, 'Well, *Sister* Bell, I'm not quite sure,' he said. 'We seem to have got ourselves into a bit of a predicament.'

He turned towards her, his face only inches from hers. And then she saw them, those chocolate eyes again. Those deep eyes. The type that drew you in and made you forget who you were and where you were. The same eyes that had mesmerised her on that long, hot night together.

'You're a distraction,' she said.

'What?'

He flinched backwards and drew his gaze away from hers and she blinked twice. Apparently she was the only person caught in the memory.

'You distracted me at work today, Cooper. It's really difficult to be in a confined space with someone you last saw naked.'

He raised an eyebrow at her candour. 'Get straight to the point, why don't you?'

'It needs to be said.' Her fingers twiddled with a lock of her hair. She was trying to appear cool and casual. 'I felt as if I couldn't concentrate at work today and that's not me. I'm *very* good at my job.'

He nodded thoughtfully. 'I'm sure you are.' He ran his hand through his hair, catching the big brown strand that fell over his eyes. He looked sideways at her and gave a grin. 'I'd hate to be responsible for your mind not being on your work.'

There it was again, that sexual tension that seemed to spring up whenever they were near each other. There was silence between them for a second as his words hung in the air. Did he really need a distraction at work? No, he didn't. What he needed was to take some time to settle into his new position and find his feet again. His eyes darted around the empty jogging track. If he didn't look at her then he couldn't think illicit thoughts. He struggled to find the words he felt he had to say. 'This is probably a bit awkward for us both.'

Melissa groaned. She raised her hand in disgust. 'Please don't give me the speech.'

This time his eyes did meet hers, and his brow furrowed in confusion.

'What do you mean—the speech?'

She shook her head. 'I'm too old for all this. It's more than a little awkward. I asked you what you did for a living. You deliberately skirted the question. Do you think I would have gone home with you if I'd known I was going to spend the next year working with you?' She was getting annoyed now. Her pent-up frustration from spending the last few hours in the labour suite with him was finally bubbling to the surface.

'Well, I don't know, do I?' he answered calmly. 'Would it have made a difference?'

Melissa gritted her teeth. What was that supposed to mean? That she would have gone home with him anyway? Did he think she was some kind of tramp?

'Yes!' she spat out. 'I've learned from experience that work and pleasure shouldn't mix.'

Did she really mean that? What she'd learnt from experience was that she, David and work shouldn't have mixed. Or maybe she just shouldn't have mixed with David, full stop. But Cooper was someone entirely new. Did she really just want to be his one-night stand? Or did she want something more? Her mind was in such a turmoil of emotions right now she didn't know what she wanted. But the last thing she needed right now was another work-related romance. Last time around it had been a disaster, with everyone knowing every detail of her life. A private life should be just that—private. She took a deep breath, trying to regain her composure, and lowered her voice. 'Please tell me you haven't told all your new colleagues about the woman you picked up in the pub?'

Cooper sat wordlessly. She thought he would do that? He'd come here to tell her that what they'd had had been a mistake. He wanted to concentrate on his new job. A beautiful stranger had seemed like a great way to move back into the land of the living. But a beautiful colleague whom he'd see on a daily basis and would imagine in all sorts of ways would only confuse things for him. His gut twisted with the inevitable realisation that he wasn't ready for this yet.

His stomach clenched into a tight knot. He lifted up his finger and brushed it momentarily against her cheek. He thought this was what he had wanted too. No complications. To forget all about it. But all of a sudden, as the woman he'd shared the most passionate night of his life with sat beside him, he wasn't so sure.

'Of course I haven't said anything to anyone,' he said softly. 'I'm not that kind of guy.'

He heard her let out a huge sigh of relief. 'Thank you, Cooper,' she whispered. She saw the hurt expression on his face and gave her shoulders a little shrug. 'I don't know you, Cooper, I mean *really* know you. I had to ask.' She leaned forward, picking up some of the red asphalt from the running track and letting it run through her fingers. 'So what happens now?'

He turned to face her. Confusion spread across his face. 'What do you mean?'

'Cooper, you came halfway across town to come and speak to me.' She put her red-tinged fingers on his arm. 'What is it you want to say?'

Her heart was thumping in her chest. She knew what she wanted him to say, but from the expression on his face she knew he would never say it.

He bit his lip. He hated this. He wasn't even sure how to say it. Maybe if he'd been here a few months and had met her at work, maybe if he'd been six months down the line and had met her in the pub, it would be different, but right now it just didn't feel right and he had to tell her. 'I'm not looking for a relationship right now.'

The words came out rapidly and for some horrible reason it had an effect on her that she hadn't expected. It hurt. She'd been taught a valuable lesson years ago when her father had left her mother for another woman, and she'd spent months watching her mother break down. With that and David, she'd learnt never to depend on a man, only on herself. And she shouldn't forget it. 'I didn't ask you for a relationship, Cooper.'

'I know that but we've got to work together and—'

Melissa stood up, she didn't need to hear any more. She patted him on the shoulder. 'Don't worry, Coop, we can work together.'

She picked up her rucksack and shrugged her shoulders into it, before glancing at her watch and starting to jog back along the track. She had

to move quickly, before the tears that were filling her eyes threatened to spill down her cheeks.
Some nights were best just forgotten.

CHAPTER THREE

COOPER glanced at his watch. It was after five o'clock and his antenatal clinic had just finished. One of his overdue patients had already been in labour when she'd come to her appointment. She hadn't even realised it and had been shocked when Cooper had sent her along to the labour ward. It had been four hours and he wanted to go and check how she was doing. But going to the labour ward meant there was a good chance that he would run into Missy.

He'd spent the best part of the last ten days avoiding the labour ward as much as possible. It wasn't as difficult as it sounded as he had patients to see in the antenatal clinics in the hospital and the community, and he had patients to see in the wards after they had delivered. He really only got called to the labour suite if there was an immediate problem and his registrar wasn't available to deal with it. The joys of being a consultant.

On the few occasions he'd attended an emergency in the labour suite, he'd managed to avoid Missy altogether. She wasn't always on duty, or was sometimes attending to another patient. But today was different. His patient would be in the medical side of the labour suite, where Missy worked. And he had already seen her in one of the corridors a few hours ago when she'd come along to the clinic to pick up some notes for a patient. He was bound to meet her today.

This was ridiculous. He couldn't let a one-night stand affect his working practice, he was far too professional for that. He stood up from his chair and strode across the room, collecting his white coat from behind the door.

His heart stopped. Just for a second. A woman, sitting in a chair, was bent over, pulling something from her bag. Her blonde hair had fallen across her face and as she sat up, she put her hands to her back and arched backwards. She was obviously pregnant, six or seven months, but that wasn't the problem.

Just for a second, just for the tiniest second, he'd thought it was Clara. The same hairstyle, the same build, even the same stage of pregnancy. He felt as if someone had stabbed him in his side. Clara, his Clara. Of course it wasn't.

He moved backwards for a minute, leaning against the door. The woman glanced at her watch then stood up as a car pulled up outside. She gathered her coat and bag and headed outside. Cooper concentrated on breathing. This wasn't the first time this had happened. When Clara had first died, he'd thought he'd seen her everywhere—crossing a road, in a supermarket, even standing at a cash dispenser. But today was different. Today felt entirely different.

A sinking realisation filled his stomach. Guilt. Today, he felt guilt. Not because he hadn't been able to save his wife, no, that guilt was firmly tucked inside and would always burrow away at him. This was an entirely new kind of guilt.

It jolted him back to reality. He'd spent the last few weeks thinking about another woman. Missy. Not his wife. Not the woman he had planned to spend the rest of his life with and who used to occupy his every waking thought. No, his thoughts had been occupied by a woman with glorious chestnut hair, stunning green eyes and a fabulous cleavage, a woman he'd spent the hottest night of his life with.

He felt sick. Sick with guilt. Was this what moving on felt like? Why had he forgotten about Clara? No, he hadn't forgotten about her, but she'd been pushed gently to the side. And he felt horrible. Horribly confused.

He dragged his mind back to the present. Patients, he had patients to see. He took a deep breath. He had a job to do and it was time to do it.

The labour suite was in full flow when he arrived. Sister Jenkins replaced the phone at the desk as he arrived. A small, rotund woman with years of experience, he'd learned that within the labour suite she was probably worth her weight in gold.

'Hi, Flora.' He smiled, leaning over the desk towards her. 'I'm looking for Maisie Kerr. I sent her along from the antenatal clinic.'

'Yes, she's in room four, progressing nicely.'

She shuffled some papers on the desk. Cooper went to start along the corridor when she spoke again. 'What about Claire Ferguson—aren't you going to see her?'

'Claire Ferguson? She's here?'

Flora nodded as she saw the surprised expression on his face. 'You didn't know?'

He shook his head. 'Where is she?'

Flora pointed down the corridor. 'Room seven in the medical suite. Melissa is looking after her.'

Cooper's face turned to stone. He had written in the patient's notes that he wanted to be informed if she was admitted for any reason. Claire Ferguson was a patient with high-risk complications of pregnancy; she was already scheduled for a Caesarean section in a few weeks' time. Claire also had some mental-health problems, which, due to her pregnancy, had caused complications as they had tried to adjust her medications. He wanted this patient treated with the most delicate of hands and was more than a little annoyed he hadn't been notified of her admission.

As he entered the room he noticed the curtains were drawn around the bed, the lights were dimmed and tranquil music was playing. When he walked in he found Melissa talking in a very low voice and gently massaging Claire's shoulders. Claire's eyes were closed and she looked calm and relaxed as Melissa continued slowly. She raised her fingers to her lips, 'Shh,' she mouthed to Cooper, and gestured for him to wait outside.

'Claire, I'm just going to leave you for a couple of minutes. Don't worry, I'll be right outside the door. Just continue with your breathing exercises and I'll be back soon.'

She adjusted the pillows on the bed, picked up the notes and followed Cooper outside.

'Didn't you see what was written on her case notes?' His voice hit her like an icy blast.

'Of course I did.'

'Then why didn't you contact me the minute Claire Ferguson was admitted?'

Melissa shook her head silently. She would never ignore something in a patient's notes. 'I asked your registrar to contact you, Dr Roberts, so I suggest you take it up with him. For your information, Claire has been admitted because her membranes have ruptured early. She was also in such an acute state of panic that I had to take the time to calm her properly before I could do an assessment of her condition.' She handed him the notes. 'I had just completed them for you. She's thirty-seven weeks' gestation. Her membrane rupture has been confirmed. She hasn't started to labour yet and will be ready to go to Theatre for her Caesarean section in the next ten minutes. The anaesthetist has been notified—I know, because I did that myself. I was just about to come and phone you to see where you were.'

Cooper lowered his eyes and attempted to open the notes but Melissa was still tightly grasping the other side. Her voice was low and steady. 'I've just spent a lot of time calming your patient to prepare her for Theatre so *don't* go in there and upset her.'

Cooper could tell by the expression on her face that she was entirely serious. What did she take him for? 'I'm not going to do that,' he said quickly, then added, 'And I will take it up with my registrar. Thank you for bringing it to my attention.'

She nodded and headed over to the midwives' station. 'Hi, Andrea, I'm just going to get my patient ready for Theatre and then I'll go for my break—is that okay?'

Andrea glanced at the disappearing coat tails of Cooper as he headed into Claire's room. 'What's up with you and Dr Hunk?'

Melissa immediately became defensive and folded her arms across her chest. 'What on earth do you mean?'

Andrea's top lip curled in indignation. 'I don't know who you think you're kidding. The pair of you prowl around each other like a pair of rival lions stalking their prey. Have you two had a tiff?'

No matter how hard she tried, Melissa could feel the colour starting to creep up her cheeks. 'No, we haven't, and I hardly know him.'

'Yeah, yeah, whatever.' Andrea's throw-away remark was coupled with a wave of her hand. She leaned forward. 'More importantly, I want to know how you're feeling. You've been looking a bit peaky lately.'

'Have I? I'm fine.' But inside she suddenly realised her colleague was right. She hadn't felt herself in quite some time. She gave a little shake of her head. 'Anyway, I'd better go and finish with Claire. I'll see you after lunch.'

Melissa headed back in to Claire, her mind spinning. Andrea was really perceptive. Had she guessed something had happened between Cooper and herself? Surely not. She had hardly seen Cooper lately. She was sure he was avoiding her. More importantly, she was furious with the way he'd just spoken to her. How dare he question her competence at work? She finished with Claire and sent the happy and calm mum-to-be off to Theatre before heading for lunch.

Lunch, however, was a spartan affair for Melissa. She sat down to the sandwiches she had brought with her, took two bites and spent the next ten minutes pushing them around the table. Was this what the mere sight of Cooper was doing to her? Putting her off her food? He could turn out to be the best diet control *ever*.

Melissa gave up and flung the sandwiches in the bin. She was never going to get her appetite back now. She normally did her injections before she ate, but because she hadn't been feeling too hungry she had waited a little longer, which was just as well as this meant she could adjust her insulin to suit her appetite.

One of the other midwives stuck her head around the door. 'Melissa, sorry to interrupt you but Dr Roberts is looking for you.'

She looked up from where she had been injecting her insulin into her stomach to see Cooper walking through the door towards her.

She quickly finished her injection and put it back in her bag. Cooper was standing next to her, looking a bit uncomfortable. 'Sorry, Melissa, I didn't mean to disturb you.'

She shook her head. 'It's all right, Cooper. Working somewhere like this, you get used to interruptions.'

He fixed her with his steady brown-eyed gaze. 'I didn't realise you were diabetic. Have you been injecting for long?'

'Since I was eight. It's like second nature to me now.' Great. She was stuck in an enclosed space yet again with Dr Hunk. Oh, my—and now she'd started using that stupid nickname. The last time her stomach had done flip-flops like this had been when she'd been a teenager and had gone to see her favourite boy band. If she could bottle and sell what she was currently feeling, she could be a millionaire.

He sat down in the chair next to her, the sleeve of his white coat brushing against her bare arm. Zing. She could practically see the sparks of electricity fly. 'Are you well controlled?'

She gave a mock look of indignation. 'That's a bit personal. Are you asking me as a professional colleague or as a friend? No, sorry that's right—we're not friends.'

'What do you mean, we're not friends?' He shifted awkwardly in his chair. Melissa was definitely taking a bit of getting used to. How could a woman who made him feel so hot under the collar put him in his place so much? She certainly never minced her words.

'Well, I hardly think we got off to the best start, did we? You purposely avoid me at work and, when we do have to work together, you can be downright rude. My "friends" don't normally behave like that around me.'

She was annoyed. He could tell because of the way her eyes were shooting sparks at him. *Lord, she was sexy.* 'Actually, I thought we got off to a great start.' His voice was very quiet, almost a whisper in the empty staffroom.

Melissa felt the hairs instantly stand up on the back of her neck in response to the implication of his words. Silence hung between them. She wasn't quite sure how to respond to that. Had she missed something?

She ignored what he'd just said and answered his original question. 'If you're asking as a *colleague* if my diabetes is well controlled then the response is, yes, it is and you don't have to worry about me being unwell while we work together. If you're asking as a *friend* then the truth is I'm a complete control freak. I check my blood sugar and adjust my insulin all the time. I want to have the best control that I possibly can.'

Cooper looked at her through thick eyelashes. 'Okay, so I feel a bit sheepish now.'

'Why?'

He cringed. 'Because I came in here to complain that you hadn't taken Claire Ferguson along to Theatre yourself. Now I realise you probably needed to get something to eat.'

She shook her head silently. 'Cooper, as a rule we never take the patients along to Theatre ourselves—unless it's an emergency. The theatre staff always come along and pick the patient up. And this...' she pulled a wrapped chocolate biscuit, which looked a little worse for wear, from her pocket for effect '...is proof that I *always* have something on standby to make sure I would never leave a patient in the lurch.' She let out a big sigh and flopped backwards in the chair. 'I was finished with Claire. I had done everything she needed and will be here waiting to receive her when she comes back from Theatre. Why are you trying to pick fault with everything I do?'

He ran his hand through his hair in frustration. 'I guess I'm just not too good at this. I've never had a relationship with someone at work before and I find the whole thing really strange. And you're right—I have been avoiding you.' He shrugged his shoulders like a scolded schoolboy.

Melissa felt her voice start to tremble. 'We don't have a relationship, Cooper. We had a one-night stand. Something that I'm not proud to admit, or that I've ever done before. It really wasn't the way I wanted to meet my new colleague. This is not something I want to do at work. And I know exactly how you feel, because I've been avoiding you too.'

'You have?' His eyes ran up and down the length of her body. This woman really didn't understand how attractive she was, did she? 'You've never had a relationship at work?' He almost couldn't believe that. If she'd worked at the last hospital he'd been a consultant at, they would practically have been jousting in the car park over her.

'That's not what I said. My ex-fiancé used to be one of the registrars here but when we split up he left, so I haven't really had to deal with any awkwardness at work before. It makes me really uncomfortable.'

So she had had a relationship at work. Why did that bother him so much? 'Why did you split up?'

Melissa shifted uncomfortably in the chair. 'David and I were together for almost three years. I wanted to start a family and he wasn't ready.'

Cooper suppressed the snort he wanted to let out. The man was obviously a fool. 'Why didn't you just wait?' It seemed like a simple enough question and it was one she'd asked herself a million times, both before and after she'd spilt up with David.

She stayed silent for a second, thinking before she answered. Only her closest friends really knew how she felt about all this. Why would she tell Cooper? Then again, Cooper had seen more of her than even her closest friends had and, truth be told, she was tired of pussy-footing round about him, watching what she said. She was exhausted. Literally exhausted. Maybe she should just tell the truth? Maybe if she did, he would run a mile. She shrugged. 'I'm twenty-nine now. I've been diabetic for twenty-one years. You know the risks for both the baby and me. Having a long-term condition like diabetes means I'm at higher risk of complications. I don't want to wait forever. I want to be healthy and I want my family to be healthy. The way that David behaved, I don't know that he would ever have been ready for a family and I didn't want to lose the opportunity by waiting to find out. I've learned in life not to depend on a man for anything.'

Wow! Why had she told him all that? From a male perspective it could look quite cold and Missy knew that. It looked as if she was just waiting for a sperm donor, rather than a loving relationship.

Cooper gave a little smile. 'But there are certain things that you just can't do on your own.' The woman really did have fire in her belly. He quirked an eyebrow at her. 'It can't really have helped, working in a maternity unit.'

She met his gaze with surprise. 'What do you mean?'

He lifted his hand and pointed to the ward outside. 'Being in here every day and seeing lots of babies being brought into the world.' He gave a guarded little smile. 'It sounds as though your biological clock is ticking so loudly it's practically thudding in your ears!'

She was stunned. Was it at his perceptiveness? Or was it his candour? Either way, what he'd just said had made her look and feel like the maddest person in the room. Why had she said anything?

Cooper was still watching her carefully. He could almost see the thoughts tearing through her brain like a washing machine on a spin cycle. For the second time he saw a sheen come over Missy's eyes. Almost automatically a fire lit up in his belly. He'd felt this way the night he'd met her. Fiercely protective. No rhyme or reason to it. He'd hit a nerve and been too forward.

'Missy, I'm sorry. Please don't be upset with me. I shouldn't have said that.'

He reached out and grasped her hand. She flinched, as if she was about to pull away, then changed her mind and stopped. It was too hard to talk. Her mind was spinning and she couldn't make sense of any of her thoughts. She'd spent a wonderful night with a gorgeous man, a man she'd never expected to see again. Now he was haunting her everyday life. Every thought she had was about him. Every time she came to work all she could think about was him. Her stomach was constantly in a knot, wondering if when she turned the next corner he would be there. And the thoughts she was having in her bed at night....

'Missy, let me fix this.' He grasped both her

hands now and turned to face her. He knew what he needed to do now, the guilt he'd felt earlier when he'd thought he'd seen Clara giving him new clarity. This was all part of moving on. Missy was the first woman he'd been attracted to in two years, and he wasn't about to let her slip from his grasp because he was behaving like an ass. 'Let's start from the beginning again. Let's have a clean slate. I like you, Missy, and I know you like me, but the reality is I hardly know you. So why don't we start from scratch?'

He stood up and put out his hand. 'Hi, pleased to meet you. I'm Cooper Roberts and I work at St Jude's as a consultant obstetrician. I think you're wildly attractive. Could I take you out for coffee some time?'

Missy's bottom lip was definitely trembling now. The unshed tears in her eyes were ready to spill down her cheeks at a moment's notice. She stretched her hand out to meet his, willing her arm to stop shaking and pushing herself up from her chair.

'Hi, I'm Melissa Bell, I'm a midwife in the labour suite at St Jude's. It's nice to meet you.'

She stopped for a second, fighting to stop herself breaking into tears.

Her eyes met his. Her heart was pounding in her chest. Everything she'd noticed about him that night was still there. His muscular build, floppy brown hair and the deep chocolate eyes that looked good enough to eat. Most of all there was just him, the man that caused continual butterflies in her chest. No man had ever had that effect on her before and she couldn't walk away from it.

'I would love to go for coffee with you, Coop.'

So why was he nervous? He'd asked her to go for coffee to try and find a way to be friends. He had to make their relationship at work easier and he was struggling with it as much as she was. Cooper had just finished fastening his deep blue shirt when his mobile rang. He glanced at the caller display, and saw it was Jake. He remembered how he'd almost told Missy his name was Jake—how embarrassing would that have made things now?

He picked up the phone. 'What's up?'

'Hi, Coop, what you up to?'

'I'm just heading out. Is something up?'

'Just wondered if you wanted to meet me for a few drinks.'

Cooper hesitated just a second too long.

'What's up, Coop? Spit it out.'

'Well, sorry, I can't. I'm meeting someone.'

'What—you've got a date?' Jake let out a wolf whistle, which reverberated down the phone and just about ruptured his eardrum.

'Calm down, Jake. It's not a date. I'm just meeting a friend for coffee.'

'Is it a female friend?'

'Yes.'

'The mystery woman you met a couple of months ago?'

'Well…yes.'

'Hate to break it to you, buddy, but that's called a date.' There was a pause for a second. 'And, Cooper?'

'Yes?'

'Good luck, it's about time.'

Cooper hung up the phone and felt himself break out into a sweat. It *was* a date, wasn't it?

He hadn't really thought of it like that. The last person he'd been out on a date with had been his wife. Somehow he didn't think his one night with Missy really counted. He stared out his window at the panoramic view of the marina. Clara had been dead for two years. They'd been married for four years, had dated for four before then, so that made...ten, ten years since he'd been out on a date. Would he even remember what he was supposed to do?

He panicked and picked up his phone. He could phone and make an excuse, say he had to go into work for something. Then it struck him. No, he couldn't. He didn't even have her mobile number.

He walked over to the window. It was a beautiful winter's day. He could see various people down at the marina among the boats. Some of them were beauties. Some of the boats must have cost more than he could earn in a lifetime. He watched one family loading up their boat with supplies. They must be going out for the day. Mum, dad and two children, both boys. They were smiling and laughing. The kids were jumping up and down, both carrying fishing rods. The mum was holding a large brown hamper—probably packed with food for the day. The dad came over and slung his arm around her shoulders, giving her a kiss on the side of the head. Cooper felt as if an arrow had pierced his heart. That should have been him. Him and Clara, with their children.

But even as he had those thoughts something shifted in his mind. That might not be his life, but why shouldn't he still have it? He'd moved to a new city, got a new job, taken his wedding ring off and decided to move on. Okay, he might have made a bit of a mess of it so far but that didn't mean that he couldn't improve things.

He tore his eyes away from the marina and marched over to the mirror. He checked his reflection quickly. Hair maybe a little too long, eyes and skin clear. He turned sideways and pulled his stomach in. Why? He didn't need to do that, he had a good physique. It was time to get back out there. He'd met a beautiful woman he was wildly attracted to. What could go wrong? With renewed vigour he picked up his jacket, glanced at his watch and headed for the door.

* * *

Melissa was almost ready. At the last count she'd changed her top four times and wiped her lipstick three times before finally settling on a cherry-red top and some lip gloss. She glanced at her watch. She'd only ten minutes to get there and her head was pounding. Was it stress? Or was the thought of meeting Cooper giving her a headache?

She picked up her brown leather bag and threw the lip gloss and a bottle of water inside. She could take some painkillers on the way. Missy opened the bathroom cabinet and started searching through what was inside. She could almost swear that these mini-bottles of lotions and potions reproduced as soon as she closed the door. Her hand hit a cardboard box and stopped her in her tracks. Tampons. When was the last time she'd used those?

The hairs on her arms stood on end. She fumbled in her bag for her diary and flicked through it. She'd had a few irregular periods and some mild symptoms so her GP had started some investigations for polycystic ovarian syndrome. So this wasn't such a big deal, was it? Her breath caught in her throat. Eight weeks. It had been eight weeks since she'd had a period. She flicked back a little further, confirming her already mounting suspicions. Even though her periods had been irregular before, there had never been a gap this long.

She felt sick. She felt physically sick. This couldn't be happening. She glanced at her watch again. There was no time. She was going to be late. She grabbed her bag and took a deep breath. This was all in her head. There was nothing to worry about. She couldn't possibly be pregnant. She'd taken every precaution. The delayed period must just be the PCOS. She glanced at her reflection in the mirror. A deathly pale face stared back. Her brain flicked into furious overtime. Did her breasts feel tender? Was this nausea something more than shock? Was she pale because she was anaemic? Missy gave herself a shake. She would pick up a pregnancy test on the way home and put her mind at rest. All this worry would be for nothing. She was sure of it.

Missy crossed the street and pushed open the door of the café. There he was, wearing blue jeans, a dark blue shirt and a black leather jacket. He looked up at her from the table where he was sitting, running his fingers through his hair. He looked nervous. Good. So was she.

'Hi, Cooper. I'm sorry I'm late. Have you been waiting long?'

She gave him an uneasy smile, fingering the gold necklace around her slim throat. She was nervous. He was relieved.

'It's fine.' He folded his newspaper and put it down on one of the chairs. 'I thought I would just come in and have a seat.'

She pulled out the chair next to her and sat down.

'What can I get you?' The voice came from a bored, slim, blonde waitress who'd already been over the table twice while Cooper had been sitting himself.

'I'll have a cappuccino and… What will you have, Missy?'

'I'll have the same.'

The waitress nodded and slopped off in the direction of the kitchen.

'So what did you do today?' he asked, leaning

across the table. She looked even more beautiful today. Her chestnut curls were pulled up on either side of her face with an ornate studded clasp. She was wearing a cherry-red top, which clung to her curves and showed a hint of her delicious cleavage. She had a little mascara on, which highlighted her green eyes, and a little lip gloss. Very natural. A passer-by might call her pretty but to Cooper she was more beautiful than any catwalk model. There was something immensely attractive about being in the company of a woman who was comfortable in her own skin.

She reached her hand up and started twiddling with one of her curls. Just like she'd been doing the first time he had seen her. 'I haven't done much this morning. I just got a little caught up at home.' That was an understatement. Her brain had been in hyperdrive all the way over here. She was beginning to imagine herself having all these pregnancy-related symptoms. Things she would never have thought about in a million years if she hadn't seen that box of tampons.

The waitress appeared again and thumped the

cups on the table, coffee sloshing onto the white saucers.

Cooper watched her retreating back. 'Service with a smile, eh?'

Melissa smiled and shrugged her shoulders sympathetically. 'She's probably in a job she hates with another hundred things on her mind. I can forgive her a little spilt coffee.'

'So why do you work on the medical side of the labour suite? I would have thought most midwives would have preferred to be on the midwifery side where they have control of the labour.'

His question caught her unawares. He couldn't possibly know what was spilling around in her mind. She took a deep breath and focused. 'I'm not "most midwives".'

He looked at her with amusement, a smile creeping across his face. 'Well, I've guessed that.'

'I usually specialise in the diabetic maternity clinic. I want to make sure women with high-risk conditions have the same rights to experience a natural birth and have control over their labour. Most of the women I see in the clinic are termed as requiring "medical care" so I try to provide some continuity for them.'

Cooper nodded thoughtfully then noticed she was pushing her coffee cup around the table. 'What's wrong—don't you like it?'

Missy gave a little grimace. 'I don't know what's wrong. I just don't have the stomach for it this morning.'

He glanced at his watch. 'Well, it's just after eleven, so why don't we make this an early lunch? You might feel better if you eat something.' He signalled to the waitress. 'I'll shout Happy Harry over to take our order.'

Food. Now she really did think she was going to throw up all over the table. 'No, don't—please.'

His head tilted to the side and his brow furrowed. 'Is everything okay, Missy?'

Missy. He'd called her Missy again and even the way he said her name made her legs turn to mush. She looked over the table at the Greek god she'd had the one-night stand with. Only he wasn't a Greek god to her any more. He was a man, with thoughts and feelings that she had to consider. He wasn't part of the fantasy dreams she'd had every night. He was a real, live person and this was supposed to be what? Their 'first proper date'? And she was about to ruin it.

'Missy, what's wrong?'

She glanced downwards. Her throat was bone dry and that coffee would be the last thing she would be swallowing. She played nervously with her fingers, refusing to lift her head and meet his gaze. It was easier this way. 'Cooper, I don't want you to panic but I'm a bit worried about something.'

'What?' He leaned forward and put his elbows on the table so he was closer to her. She looked awful and why wasn't she looking at him? What was she going to say?

'I think…I mean, I'm not sure…well, I think there could be a possibility that I might be pregnant.'

There, she'd said it. She watched as the colour drained from his face and he sat back in his chair.

'Oh.'

'That's all you've got to say? Oh?'

'You took me by surprise. I mean, I know there

was an issue with the condom, but I thought you were going to go and get—'

'I did.'

'You did?' His voice rose, almost hopefully, it seemed.

'Yes, I did, but we both know it's not foolproof.'

He sighed and put his hand across the table and took her hand. 'But it's been weeks. Surely you would have missed a few periods by now?

She nodded. 'Normally I probably would have. But I've been having investigations for PCOS as my periods have been really irregular. And because I'd taken the morning-after pill I just assumed everything was fine. It wasn't until today that I realised how long it had been since I'd had a normal period.'

He nodded slowly, taking in everything she's just said. 'How are you feeling?'

'Right now, awful.' Her eyes met his and he could see the worry and confusion in her face. 'I don't know if I'm imagining symptoms for myself. On the way over here I seem to have given myself every pregnancy symptom in the world.'

Somewhere deep inside her head a voice was screaming. *Baby! Baby!* Pregnancy was measured from the date of the last proper period so, if she was expecting, that would make her between ten and eleven weeks pregnant. The realisation made the hairs on her arms stand on end.

Cooper pushed his cup away. 'Why don't we find out?'

Melissa felt sick. 'What do you mean?'

'Let's go and get a test. You could do it now.'

Everything about this seemed wrong. 'This isn't a spectator sport.' If she was going to do a pregnancy test, she wanted to do it in private. More than that, she needed some time alone to think. What on earth was she going to do? This was supposed to have been a 'starting again, getting to know you' date, not a 'guess who might be pregnant' date. She couldn't believe this was happening.

'I've got as much right to know as you have.' His voice was low and firm. He was watching her with those brooding brown eyes. The ones that still made her heart leap. The ones that got her into this situation in the first place.

'I know that,' she whispered. Lunch was forgotten. The nice, quiet meeting for coffee was forgotten. Their first official date was forgotten. Everything paled into insignificance next to this. Why this? Why now?

Cooper signalled to the waitress for their bill. He thrust his hand deep into the pocket of his jeans to pull out some money and sent coins scattering across the floor. Melissa bent down to help him retrieve them and froze. Something glistened at her from the dark-tiled floor. There was no mistaking it. A gold wedding band.

Cooper hadn't noticed as he was picking up coins from under his chair. 'I'm such a klutz,' he muttered, gathering up the coins and sitting back down in the seat opposite. The waitress thumped the bill down on the table and walked away. Cooper watched her retreating back. 'Well, I guess we won't be leaving a tip for the service.'

Melissa hadn't moved. She couldn't believe it. Every hair on her body stood on end, the nerve endings instantly intensified. She could feel bile rise in the back of her throat. Any moment now she was going to be physically sick. She reached out her hand and dropped the gold wedding band onto the table.

Silence. Silence was golden, that's what they said. On this occasion, silence was a gold wedding band.

She could see the pain. It was written all over his face. 'I can explain.'

'You'd better.' Please, no. Please, don't let me have bedded a married man. Please, don't let me find out that I'm pregnant by a man who has a wife and 2.4 children stashed away somewhere.

'I'm a widower.'

Wow! She hadn't been expecting that.

He turned the ring over and over in his hand. 'My wife died two years ago.' His voice was trembling now. That hadn't been there before. This was still raw. 'I've only recently taken my wedding ring off, but I still keep it in my pocket. That was part of the reason why I came here.' He lifted his heavy eyelids and looked at her through thick dark lashes. 'To start anew. None of the people I work with here know I'm a widower. It saves too many difficult questions.'

Melissa nodded. She still hadn't spoken. A widower, well, it was better than a married man. Her heart reached out to him. He was obviously still grieving. But her head screamed at her. She could be pregnant by a man who was still grieving for his dead wife. A man who still carried his wedding ring in his pocket. A man who obviously wasn't ready to move on.

'Say something.'

Melissa stood up and picked up her bag. 'I've got a lot to think about. I'll let you know what happens.'

'Are you going to do a test?'

'Obviously.'

'Can I be there?'

'No.'

He stood up. 'I'm sorry, Missy. This is my fault. I've put you in this position. Let me be there for you. Don't do the test alone.'

The words echoed around her head. How could he be there for her? He still carried his wedding ring in his pocket.

'Cooper, I just don't know. I think I should do this on my own. This might all be a panic over nothing.'

'Then let's find out.' His voice was calm and steady and he reached over and took her hand. She hesitated for a second. He did have the right to know. He wasn't married, he wasn't cheating on anyone, he just wasn't *hers*, and this was not how she'd imagined having a family. But it was time to be an adult. And it was time to find out.

It took ten minutes to find a pharmacy, buy a test and get home.

Missy was desperate to pee and didn't want to waste the opportunity. She might be a midwife but she'd no idea there were so many different kinds of pregnancy tests. She was so used to the one that they used routinely in the hospital that the array of boxes had bewildered her. In the end Cooper had grabbed the first two that he'd seen and paid for them, while she'd still stood there, dithering.

A quick glance at the instructions and she headed for the toilet. She looked at her watch. Who knew two minutes could be so long?

She'd wanted a child for so long. But she'd wanted the loving relationship that went with having a child. At least in her mind it did. She was twenty-nine. She'd been diabetic for twenty-one years. She didn't want to wait any longer. She wasn't going to.

She glanced at her watch. One minute up.

Cooper was standing, glancing out of her window, with his hands deep in his pockets. He didn't seem to be looking at his watch. He seemed lost in another world. She couldn't really have picked a worse candidate for a father. Would an anonymous one-night stand have been better? She was going to have to see Cooper at work every day. Would he interfere in her life? Would he want to have contact with her baby? *Her baby.* She was already starting to think that way.

Her eyes glanced across the counter as Cooper came and sat next to her. They didn't have to wait a whole two minutes. He'd bought the most expensive test on the market. This one didn't have pink or blue lines. This one told it like it was.

One word. *Pregnant.*

CHAPTER FOUR

COOPER looked at the test. He felt as if he were in a bad dream. What was she thinking about? A chill came over his body. Melissa had told him that she wanted a baby, but what if she didn't want *his* baby?

Melissa was a wonderful woman, almost a tonic for the two previous years. She was beautiful, and dedicated to her job. She was independent, not clingy. She understood the pressures of work and the problems they could cause for someone like him. Who knows where this could have led? Maybe she would have been a stepping stone for him. A nice way to ease back into the land of dating. Maybe he would have grown to love her and their relationship would have deepened. Maybe she would only ever have been a one-night stand. But now…

He had to ask the question. 'What do you want to do?'

She looked stunned. 'What do you mean?'

'Do you want to have the baby?'

His words came out colder, harsher than he had meant them to. The timing was a disaster. An unexpected pregnancy. They hadn't had a chance to get to know each other, to develop any potential relationship, and now a pregnancy? Cooper felt ill. Then, to top it all off, there had been the wedding-ring incident. Her face had been unreadable. He'd no idea what she thought about that. Was she angry with him? Upset?

He'd told her about Clara. But he hadn't told her about Lily, his daughter. Even her name brought pain to his heart. His perfect baby who should have been pink and screaming had been blue and quiet. He couldn't even bear to think about it. He wasn't ready to talk about her yet. Melissa was pregnant, how could he tell her his wife had died due to pregnancy complications? How could he tell her his baby had died too? It would frighten her, terrify her even. He couldn't do that. Their relationship wasn't stable enough for that.

'Why on earth would you think I wouldn't want this baby?' Her hands flew automatically to her stomach in a protective gesture. Her eyes seemed wide and afraid. She was protecting her baby, *their baby*. And another range of wild thoughts flew through his head.

Melissa was diabetic. Making her more at risk of complications than others. Could he really support her through a pregnancy? Could he watch her body change shape and see the little life grow under her skin, while the whole time he would be terrified something would happen again?

He hesitated. 'I'm just not sure, Melissa. Truth be told, I don't know what you want.'

And he didn't know what he wanted either. Pregnancy had brought the whole world into perspective for him. A tight fist clenched around his heart as he thought about his daughter. He couldn't go through that again. *Get a grip, Cooper!*

This was his second chance. He couldn't possibly walk away—he wasn't that kind of man. He would support her, he would help her. He would do anything possible to make sure this time his child made it into the world alive. It was his job, his duty and his responsibility. His heart? Well, it would just have to be put to the side right now. Facts he could deal with, emotions would just have to wait.

Melissa was in shock. She was still sitting in the same position with her hand on her stomach. She still couldn't believe this was happening. She'd always wanted to be a mother. But her dreams of being a mother had always gone alongside dreams of a happy family, a family that involved a father, something she'd been deprived of. This wasn't how she had imagined finding out she was pregnant—in her house with a man she'd had a one-night stand with.

And how on earth could Cooper think that she might not want this baby? She could never ever not want this baby. But maybe this wasn't about her, maybe this was about him?

She took a deep breath, 'Do *you* want to have this baby?'

Her voice brought him into check. 'Of course I do, Melissa.'

She nodded in relief at his words. He'd said what she needed to hear.

But her head was spinning. Where would Cooper fit into this equation? When her father had left, she'd vowed never to rely on a man for anything. Her mother had been left financially and emotionally bereft. Even in her relationship with David, she'd kept her own flat, her own finances, which in the end, had turned out to be just as well. Because he had left too.

But now that she knew they both wanted this baby, her mind flew off at a tangent. She knew that her long-term diabetes control was good. And she knew that was one of the key factors influencing her baby's health. But she hadn't been planning a pregnancy so she hadn't taken any folic-acid supplements or watched what she had been eating. Could these things affect her baby? What if she'd done something that could have damaged her developing baby?

'I need to know if this baby's okay.' Tears pricked her eyes and her voice was so quiet it was barely a whisper.

'What?' Cooper was a little stunned by her words.

'I need to know, Cooper.' She lifted her heavy lids to meet his gaze. 'I didn't plan this pregnancy, I haven't been taking folic acid. You know that I'm at higher risk of just about everything. What if something is wrong with this baby because I didn't know I was pregnant?'

He could hear the panic in her voice as it rose in pitch. He was an obstetrician. He could understand her feelings, her panic. She was only vocalising what he'd thought about a few moments before. He walked around the counter and put his arm around her shoulders. 'Calm down, Missy. You have no reason to worry like that, do you?' His voice was calm. 'You told me yourself that you're a control freak.' His hand rubbed her arm in reassurance. 'So I'm imagining that your blood-glucose levels will have been good and your baby won't have been put at any greater risk.'

She looked lost in thought but nodded almost absentmindedly.

'Do you want me to arrange a scan appointment

for you? Will that make you feel a little better? I could do it in the next few days.'

'Could you?' Her head turned anxiously towards his.

'Of course I could.' He gave her a little smile and planted a kiss on her forehead. 'It's one of the perks of the job.'

'As soon as I visit the scan room everyone will know that I'm pregnant—there's no secrets in that place.' She could almost hear the jungle drums in her head.

He nodded his head. 'I know that,' he said. 'I'm not worried.'

She hesitated. 'It's just that…I understand why you might not have wanted people at work to know you were widowed. I can appreciate you wanting to keep parts of your life private. But now, with this…' Her hands pointed towards her belly.

Cooper nodded. 'Let me worry about that, Melissa.'

He wrapped his arms around her and they stood, locked together. He'd spent the last two years staying away from personal issues that he couldn't have control over—it had been the only thing that had kept him sane. But for the second time in his life Cooper felt that certain elements were spiralling out of his grasp. Could he survive again?

Melissa tapped her foot impatiently on the waiting-room floor. Cooper was sitting next to her in jeans and a jumper, his white coat left in the confines of his office. She wasn't going to let him play the 'I work here' card today. Today she wanted them to be normal parents-to-be. Everything else had to be left at the door.

She sipped at the plastic cup of water in her hand. Her bladder was about to burst. It was all very well, telling mums-to-be they had to have a full bladder to get the best possible view on their scan, it was quite another to try and consume four cups of chilled water.

'Melissa Bell?' The sonographer stood at the entrance to the waiting room, her eyes peering into the gloomy room. 'Oh, it is you; I thought I recognised the name. Come on in.'

She came over, gave Melissa's hand a little

squeeze and led the way to the darkened scan room. Melissa had known Fiona for over seven years. She was always completely professional and there wasn't a flicker of surprise on her face as Cooper followed them into the small space.

'You know the drill, Melissa. Get yourself up on the couch and we'll see if I can show you this baby.'

Melissa lay up on the paper-covered couch and loosened her jeans. Her heart started beating frantically in her chest. She took a deep breath. She'd accompanied many women to their scans before, but this was different. She wasn't here as a midwife, she was here as a patient. Everything suddenly had a new perspective for her. Cooper pulled out the chair next to her and sat down. His eyes were fixed entirely on the blank screen.

Fiona checked the card she'd been given. She gave Melissa a little smile. 'Well, I don't need to check your name with you. Are you still at the same address?' Melissa nodded silently. 'And with the same GP? Good. Okay, I'm going to put a little gel on your stomach. I did try to warm it up, so it shouldn't be too cold.'

Melissa inhaled sharply as the gel squirted onto her stomach. *Please, let everything be all right.* Fiona positioned the transducer and started moving it across Melissa's abdomen. She moved down a little lower and pressed firmly.

Melissa heard the noise before she recognised the shape on the screen. A small, rapid heartbeat. As clear as could be. Melissa felt a grin spread across her face and a sense of relief stretch through her body. Fiona started to point at the screen. 'Look, here we are. There is baby's heart—look at the flicker on the screen.'

Melissa nodded enthusiastically. She couldn't speak. She couldn't wipe the smile off her face.

Fiona adjusted the transducer and started to take some measurements. 'Look, there's the baby's head, femur, and the baby's arm. And, oh, it looks as if baby is trying to wave at us!' She shot Melissa a huge smile. 'How far along did you think you were?' She looked down and glanced at the white card again, answering her own question. 'About eleven weeks?'

Melissa felt her breath catch in her throat. *Was something wrong? Did the dates not match?*

Fiona's voice was loud and clear, banishing any bad thoughts. 'Well, you're almost spot on. Eleven weeks and four days, according to this scan. And everything looks great.' She took down a few notes before trying to get a good image of the baby.

Melissa squirmed uncomfortably as the pressure on her abdomen mounted. She didn't want to move but she desperately needed to go to the toilet. Fiona shot her a knowing smile. 'I'll just be second. There, now, baby's in just the right position. I take it you want the nuchal translucency scan done?'

Melissa glanced over at Cooper and gave a nod. The nuchal translucency test was a simple scan that, used with the age of the baby and the age of the mother, gave an estimated risk of the baby having Down's syndrome. It was yet another thing she was at higher risk of.

Fiona spent a few seconds measuring the fluid at the back of the baby's neck and recording her results. 'This scan picture, along with your details and your blood test, will go up to the central lab. Your test results will take about two weeks. Okay?'

Melissa nodded gratefully, thankful her baby had been lying in the correct position for the scan. She didn't know how much longer her bladder was going to last.

Fiona swept the transducer across her abdomen. 'I want to get a good picture for you.'

A few seconds later she pressed a button on the screen and a little black and white image printed out for Melissa.

'And one for Dad?'

Silence. Melissa turned. In the darkened room she had to screw her eyes up to see Cooper's face. It hadn't moved. He was still staring at the screen.

Cooper felt as if the black walls were closing in around him. The only light in the room came from the monitor in front of him. There was his baby. Alive, on the screen. He'd been here before. He'd attended three scans with Clara and watched his daughter grow before his eyes. Until, one day, she was gone. Nothing. He focused on the flickering heartbeat on the screen, which gave him reassurance that this baby was alive and developing just as it should. He knew the problems diabetes could cause for a developing foetus—hell, he could write a book on them. But everything looked good. They wouldn't really know for sure until the detailed scan around twenty weeks but right now his child was alive and growing. He should feel comforted, relieved. Instead, he just felt sick with worry. What if something went wrong again?

'Cooper?' Missy reached out and touched his hand. He started.

'What? Oh, yes….yes, sorry, Fiona. Yes, can I have a picture please?'

He watched as the little picture printed out and Fiona tore it off and handed it to him. Fiona wiped the remaining gel from Missy's abdomen. She leapt up and ducked into the strategically placed toilet leading off the scanning room.

Instant. Relief. Her eyes fell to the image of her baby, enclosed in a little plastic envelope, which she'd placed up next to the sink. Magic. After all these years, she really was going to have a baby. Her hands began to tremble. This was real.

She didn't care what anyone else thought, or how Cooper fitted into this equation. She could do this. She could do this on her own. She washed her hands and went back to meet Cooper.

He was still outside, talking to Fiona. 'So the expected date of delivery will be the 4th of October?'

Fiona nodded. 'Finished, Melissa? Good. Come over here and I'll set up appointment times for the rest of your scans. I take it you'll be attending the diabetic antenatal clinic?'

Melissa nodded in response.

'In that case, Dr McPherson likes all his ladies to have a scan every month to check for growth and development, but you know that, don't you? I'll also give you a time for your detailed scan at twenty-one weeks. We've got a new state-of-the-art scanner. It gives 3D images of the baby's face. You'll love it.'

Melissa nodded enthusiastically as Fiona wrote down the appointment times on a card for her.

Cooper was standing in the corner of the room. His eyes were fixed on the little photograph in front of him. She watched him. He was breathing in slowly through his nose and blowing the air back out in a steady stream through his lips. It was a control exercise. Some women used it when they were in labour. Others used it to stop panic attacks or control temper.

Chills ran down Melissa's spine. How well did she really know this man? Why on earth would a consultant obstetrician, a man who looked at baby scans all day, need to practise a control technique when looking at a scan of their baby?

She took the card being proffered by Fiona. 'That was great, Fiona, thanks very much.' She went to walk out of the scanning room but Fiona placed a hand on her arm, her eyes glancing over to where Cooper stood. 'You know if you're ever concerned at all, about anything, scan appointment or not, just come and see me. I'll always fit you in if you have any worries.'

Melissa nodded appreciatively, refusing to even look back towards Cooper. 'I know, Fiona, and thank you.'

She lifted her bag from the floor and took off down the corridor at a brisk pace. She should be on top of the world right now. Maybe it wasn't an ideal situation, but it certainly wasn't the worst. She pushed her scan picture into her handbag. She would look at it again later, when she didn't feel as if the weight of the world was pressing down on her shoulders. Her eyes began to fill up. *No! Dash these hormones!*

Cooper appeared at her elbow. 'Melissa, slow down.' He grabbed her arm, halting her steps and turning her around to face him. 'What's wrong?'

She couldn't help it. All her frustrations were jumbled up in her brain, she couldn't translate them into words, and before she knew it, tears were streaming down her face.

Cooper's face fell. He knew this was his fault and he enveloped her in a bear hug in the middle of the hospital corridor. 'Everything was fine, Missy.' He stroked the hair at the back of her neck. 'You know the baby is healthy. Don't be upset.'

'Don't be upset!' She landed both hands on his chest and pushed him away fiercely. 'What was wrong with you in there?' She spat the words out through gritted teeth. 'You've just ruined what should have been one of the happiest moments of my life. You sat in there as if you were waiting for an executioner—not seeing your baby for the first time. What on earth was wrong with you? I wish I'd never asked you to come!'

All her frustration came bubbling to the surface. She'd seen her baby now and everything about this seemed so *real*. She'd had a one-night stand, with someone she didn't know that well and apparently didn't understand, and now she was paying the price. It didn't matter to her if she and Cooper didn't have a relationship—she wasn't going to get the happy husband and the house with the white picket fence. But she wanted her baby to have a relationship with its father. She didn't just want him to be a name on a birth certificate. She wanted her baby to be loved. *To be wanted.*

After her father had left, Melissa had never seen him again. She'd only received a few letters and birthday cards. The feeling of desertion in her had been enormous. And she *never* wanted her child to feel like that.

Cooper struggled to find words. It was so easy to be a doctor and look at other people's baby scans. Even when they were filled with bad news, he was there as the professional, the person to guide and advise. This was *so* different. This was his child. A child he wanted to protect from all harm and keep safe. He wanted to be in control. But he wasn't and he didn't know how to tell her—without telling her why he was so scared and probably terrifying her to death and giving her sleepless nights.

He shook his head. 'Don't say that, Missy. Look, I can't explain right now, but I found it quite hard, okay?' He looked about him. They were standing in the middle of a hospital corridor, hardly the time or the place for the thoughts that were circulating in his mind.

'But it shouldn't be hard, Cooper. It should be happy. This should be a happy time for you and for me. We get to see our baby's heartbeat for the first time, we should be shouting from the rooftops!'

'I know that and I am happy, I am.'

'No, Cooper, you're not, and I don't understand. You're an obstetrician—you see hundreds of scans—why on earth couldn't you conjure up a bit of happiness at seeing your baby for the first time?' She was clearly getting agitated and this was the last thing he wanted. 'You told me you wanted this baby. But it didn't seem like that in there. I know this wasn't planned. I know this probably shouldn't have happened. But do you know what? I'm glad. I'm glad this happened. Even if you're not.'

It was the first time Cooper had ever heard her shout. And from the concerned looks from the some of the staff members passing in the corridor, it was obviously the first time they had heard her shout too. Her face was scarlet with anger, hot tears dropping in large splotches onto the corridor floor.

Cooper had that horrible feeling of everything being out of his control again. If this was a nice tale he would take her by the hand and tell her how he'd felt in that scan room, because this wasn't the first time he'd seen his child's heartbeat, it was the second. But that would involve a long, convoluted story about how he'd lost his wife and child through a pregnancy complication. And what kind of man would that make him? This wasn't a nice story, this was real life, for him and for Missy and their baby. If Missy was stressed now, that could only make her ten times worse.

How the hell had he got himself into this mess? He pulled a handkerchief from his pocket and handed it to her. 'I think you're overreacting. Calm down.' He knew that he was being condescending and he knew he shouldn't do it. But right now he couldn't handle the demons in his head. And he wasn't going to try and pretend to be perfect. 'Go and get something to eat and I'll see you later.'

As if conjured up by magic, Andrea appeared. She shot Cooper a look that should have flayed him. Her voice was quiet and steady. 'Missy, are you all right?' She took Melissa gently by the arm and led her down the corridor towards the staffroom. A single shake of her head told Cooper not to follow.

And for the first time ever he didn't want to.

CHAPTER FIVE

'CONGRATULATIONS, Sister Bell.'

'Sorry?' Melissa was startled by the voice behind her at the conference. Had someone guessed she was pregnant? She glanced down at her stomach—definitely nothing obvious there. She was due her results from her combined nuchal scan and blood test in the next day or so, but didn't think she'd started to show yet. She had just presented a paper on midwifery management of high-risk pregnancies. Cooper was with her today and had headed off in the direction of the refreshments to get her something to eat. She turned to face the woman behind her. A short, blonde, rotund woman with a friendly expression. 'I'm sorry,' said Melissa again as she turned in her chair. 'Have we met?'

The woman wedged herself in the chair next to Melissa. Melissa gave a little smile as she recognised the designer linen suit being rumpled beyond all recognition.

The woman followed her eyes and smiled. 'I hate this suit,' she sighed, pulling at the cream material. 'Linen crushes at the slightest touch but it was the only thing I could fit into this morning.' She put out her hand towards Melissa. 'I must look like a bag lady but I'm Karen Connelly, one of the obstetricians at St Benjamin's in Leeds. I wanted to congratulate you on your paper.'

'Oh, thanks very much.' Missy felt a wave of relief as she realised the woman had no idea she was pregnant and was only a fellow professional here to discuss the paper.

Karen Connelly glanced over her shoulder, her messy blonde hair almost catching Melissa in the face. She gave a little smile as she saw Cooper approaching, precariously balancing two steaming cups and two plates loaded with food. 'I see you're here with Cooper.'

A strange sensation shot straight to the front of Missy's mind as she caught the expression on Karen Connelly's face. Was this woman interested in Cooper? Something twisted in her gut. Was that jealousy? You bet it was.

Watching him cross the room, she could see women's heads turning in appreciation of his lithe frame. He was dressed in a dark grey suit, crisp white shirt and red silk tie, and looked hot. The mere thought of him made her skin prickle. It had been a strange week. She was almost beginning to believe that he was right, that maybe she had overreacted outside the scan room. But something still niggled away at her, something she just couldn't put her finger on.

Cooper reached the table, his head still down and deep in concentration as he placed the cups and plates on the table. He gave a triumphant smile as he lifted his eyes to Melissa. A smile that spread even further when he saw who was sitting next to her.

'Coop, hi, it's lovely to see you again.' Karen pushed herself up and wrapped her arms around Cooper's neck, kissing him on both cheeks. 'It's been far too long.'

Cooper returned the kisses and sat down next to Missy, pushing one of the plates in her direction. 'It's great to see you too. What are you doing here?'

She waved her arm towards Missy. 'Oh, I just came over to congratulate your Sister Bell on her presentation.'

Cooper nodded and took a drink of his coffee. 'That was nice of you, Karen.' He turned towards Missy. 'See, Missy, I told you your presentation was fine.' He turned back to Karen. 'She was up half the night, worrying about it.'

Karen raised her eyebrow at Cooper and gave him a wide smile, 'And how would you know that, Cooper?'

Cooper, who was in mid-sip of his coffee, coughed and spluttered. 'Well, what I meant was…that she told me,' he finished quickly as colour flooded into his cheeks.

Missy smiled. She'd never seen Coop blush before, and it was quite endearing. He was quite right—she had told him. But there was something kind of nice about Karen thinking it meant something else entirely.

Karen patted his arm and smiled at Missy. 'Cooper, don't get yourself in a state, I was only teasing. But…' she glanced between him and Missy '…I'm really glad that I hit the nail on the head, whether by accident or not.' She stood up and turned around. putting her hand out towards Missy. 'It's a pleasure to meet you, Missy, and I hope things work out well between you.'

Missy gave her a little smile as she shook the outstretched hand.

Karen bent over and kissed Cooper on the cheek again as she gave his shoulder a squeeze. 'I'm so happy that you finally got back on the wagon, Cooper. After Clara and Lily, it's so nice to see you've met someone new.' She gave them a little wave. 'I'll leave you both to eat your lunch and hopefully will see you both later.' She walked off across the conference hall, leaving destruction in her wake.

Missy hadn't moved. She hadn't even blinked. Cooper had just been about to take a bite from a sausage roll and his mouth remained open as the sausage roll hovered at his lips.

Neither of them said anything. Melissa felt as if she'd been punched. The air in the room felt heavy, claustrophobic. Melissa felt a wave of nausea sweep over her and pushed the plate of food away untouched. She could feel him staring at her, waiting for her to react, to say something. But they were in the middle of a conference room with hundreds of other delegates—was this really the place for this discussion?

She could feel fury building in her chest. She hadn't imagined anything last week. She hadn't overreacted outside the scan room.

Her eyes met his. The shutters were still there. She couldn't live like this. Her hands were automatically positioned on her stomach in a protective manner. It was bad enough finding out that Cooper was widowed and still carried his wedding ring in his pocket. What else was she about to find out? She couldn't bring this baby into the world without having all the facts.

Melissa felt the tremble in her voice as she said the words, 'What do you have to tell me, Cooper?'

Her voice got stronger, steadier as her determination grew. 'You owe me, Cooper. You owe me and our baby. We have a right to know.'

The silence was suffocating. But Melissa was determined not to break it. She needed answers.

The strain was visible on his face. He looked as if his heart had been broken in two. The sausage roll finally managed to make its way back down to the table and onto a plate. She could see him taking a few deep breaths. Karen's words started to settle in her brain where tiny little connections began to be made.

'Who is Lily, Cooper? And what happened to Clara?'

His worry lines had never looked so deep. The circles under his eyes had never been so dark.

'Clara…' He sucked in a deep breath, his eyes meeting hers in a steady gaze. 'She was pregnant when she died. Thirty-nine weeks. Our daughter Lily was stillborn.'

Melissa felt as if she had just run headlong into a brick wall. Oxygen left her body but didn't seem to come back in. Almost instantly every hair on her body stood on end, hypersensitive to their surroundings. The blood was pounding in her veins, she could feel her heart thudding in her chest. She struggled to speak. 'Wh...? What? What happened? Was it an accident?'

Cooper shook his head and reached out his hand to her. 'Clara had a PE.'

'A PE?' Her words were whispered, almost inaudible. A pulmonary embolism, or a clot in the lungs, was an unusual complication of pregnancy. 'Was she unwell? Did she have an underlying condition that caused it?' A thousand questions spun around in her mind.

He pulled his hand back from hers. His face was so pale it almost looked translucent. 'No, Missy. Clara had no underlying conditions. She had no major accidents beforehand, she hadn't even been off her feet for a few days. She became unwell really quickly, had shortness of breath and phoned for an ambulance herself. She'd tried to call me but I was in Theatre and she left me a message. By the time I got to the emergency department she was almost unconscious.' The words were staccato, coming out in short, sharp bursts. He ran his hand through his hair and stared over Missy's shoulder at a fixed point on the wall. 'My wife and daughter died because I missed something that cost them their lives.'

'Cooper, you can't possibly think—'

He cut her off with an ice-cold, almost blank stare. 'It turned out Clara had banged her leg a few days before. It seemed so unimportant that she hadn't even told me about it. Even when it *must* have been hurting her the next day and the day after, when the clot was forming in her leg.' The frustration he felt was evident.

She tried to suck in air. Her brain was racing. How could he not tell her something like this? In her mind, tiny pieces of the jigsaw puzzle started to fall into place. His flat had no family pictures on display. The wedding ring he still carried in his pocket. The way he'd acted in the scan room. Cooper wasn't ready to move on. It wasn't just that he wasn't ready for a relationship, it almost seemed as if he wasn't ready to have a life again. And now she understood why.

It felt like a betrayal. He'd misled her. He'd let her think that this was his first child, his first experience of having a partner who was pregnant.

'You should have told me.' Melissa shook her

head. She was having trouble taking all of this in. Her head was swimming with a million questions that really couldn't be shouted across a busy conference room. She went to stand up and felt herself sway.

Cooper was at her side in an instant, his arm around her waist, supporting her weight on her unsteady legs. 'Missy, are you okay? God, I'm so sorry.' He looked frantically around the room until he spotted the nearest exit. 'Let's get out of here and get some fresh air. Can you manage?'

She nodded and walked with him, hating the fact her legs had turned to jelly and her head felt as if a thousand butterflies were flapping their wings inside it.

A welcome blast of cool air hit her as soon as they stepped outside the main doors into the reception area. Cooper's arm was still around her and he guided her over to some nearby comfortable sofas next to the bar. 'Can I get you something to drink?'

'Just some soda water, please.'

She took a few moments to gather her thoughts while he stood at the bar. He came back with a tray with two glasses, a bowl of soup and some crusty bread.

'Sorry,' he said apologetically, 'it was all they had. You never got a chance to eat in there—do you think your blood sugar could be low?'

She pulled her glucose meter from her bag and took a few seconds to prick to her finger and test her blood. 'I don't much feel like eating, Cooper.'

The machine buzzed and he sat down next to her, rather than at the other side of the table, looking over her shoulder at the result.

'Eat, Missy. This can wait until you feel a bit better.'

She knew he was right and it annoyed her. She didn't like anyone telling her what to do. She liked to control her diabetes and make her own decisions regarding her care. But she didn't just have herself to think about any more. She lifted the spoon to her mouth and reluctantly began to eat.

Cooper waited a few minutes until she'd finished, his hands turning over and over in his lap. 'Melissa, I couldn't tell you.' He gestured towards her stomach. 'How could I?'

'How could you not?' Her voice was low and steady but did nothing to disguise the anger she was feeling.

Cooper's face contorted. 'How could I tell you? You were worried enough about being pregnant, being diabetic and the possible effects on the baby. I couldn't tell you my wife had died due to a complication of pregnancy and that our daughter was stillborn. How insensitive would that have been?'

'You should have told me.' Her voice was firmer now as the jumbled thoughts became firmer in her mind. 'That's why you were strange in the scan room, wasn't it? I thought you were seeing your baby for the first time, but now I realise that you weren't. You'd done all this before.' How dare he not tell her something as important as this? She didn't think how her words might hurt him, she was too upset to give his feelings a second thought. Then another notion jumped into her head as realisation took hold.

'I must be your worst nightmare.'

Cooper looked stunned. 'What? What are you

talking about?' He ran his hands through his hair in frustration.

'When I told you I was pregnant. It must have been your worst nightmare.' Her mind went into overdrive. She pointed a finger at him accusingly. 'You already had one wife who'd died with pregnancy complications and then you get me!' She gestured towards her barely extended abdomen. 'A diabetic who is at higher risk of just about everything!'

Cooper was silent, as if he didn't know how to respond. And in her mind that was enough. He agreed with her, but couldn't put those thoughts into words.

The thoughts continued to form in her mind. Cooper fumbled. He tried to speak but Melissa cut him off.

'This is impossible. This is never going to work. I can't get my head around any of this.' A single tear slid down her cheek and she hurriedly brushed it away. She looked at the man who made her blood race through her veins and her heart pound furiously. She was wildly attracted to him and easily in danger of falling in love with him. She'd never felt anything like this before.

But he couldn't possibly love her. They could never be a family while he was still mourning the loss of his wife and child. And the cold, harsh reality was that Missy wanted everything. She wanted what she'd never had. She wanted the beautiful baby and the beautiful husband to go with it.

Her hands ran over her stomach. Did he even want this baby?

Cooper watched the turmoil of emotions flash across Missy's face. She was in pain and this was his fault. Only he could fix this.

He placed one hand over hers on her stomach and used the other to lift her chin towards him.

'Missy, I'm glad that you know. This wasn't the best way for you to find out but now it means all my cards are on the table and there are no secrets between us.'

'Do you even want this baby, Cooper?' she whispered.

'Yes, absolutely.' His voice was resolute with

no hesitation. 'Missy, I've already lost one child, this baby means everything to me.'

Her heart sank. He hadn't mentioned her. He'd only mentioned the baby.

'But what about me?' Her eyes searched his face. She had to ask the question. She had to prepare herself for the worst. 'Do you want me too?'

His eyes dropped from her face. 'Missy, I'm not going to tell you any lies. I'm only ever going to tell you the truth. And the truth is I don't know. I'm not ready to make that decision yet.' His hands were trembling and she could see he was struggling with this but that didn't make his answer any easier to take.

'What I can promise you is that I'm going to be with you every step of the way in this pregnancy. I guarantee it.'

Missy nodded numbly. Her child may be secure and loved, but what about her?

CHAPTER SIX

MISSY stuffed her bag into her locker and took a quick glance in the mirror to check her appearance. She had a glow. She'd put a little fake tan on her face and arms last night to take away her deathly pale complexion, but there was something else. She gave herself a little smile before turning and heading out the door.

The labour suite had a whole new meaning for her now. In around twenty-five weeks she would be a patient, not a member of staff. She was sure about what she wanted to do now. Her work colleagues had been great, all very supportive, and they were currently fighting over who got to deliver her baby. She could take up to a year off and when she wanted to return to work she knew the hospital had good crèche facilities. The only thing she hadn't worked out was where Cooper fitted into this equation. Word got round quickly in maternity units and everyone already knew that Cooper had attended the scan with her.

Melissa headed down to the midwives' station and took a quick glance at the whiteboard, which showed how many patients were in the unit and which midwife they were allocated to. Today she was in the medical unit, taking charge of the pre- and post-op mums. The theatre list was hanging at the side of the desk. Only two women were due for Caesarean sections today, both of whom weren't due to go to Theatre until after lunchtime. It could be a quiet day for her.

Melissa went along to the pre- and post-op room for a handover from the midwife due to go off duty.

'Hi, Sally, what have you got for me?'

'Hey, Melissa. Both ladies are ready for Theatre. Julie Bates is forty-one and a primipara. She's thirty-seven weeks' gestation and is being sectioned due to placenta praevia. Wendy Kerr is twenty-two and is a para plus one, currently thirty-nine weeks' gestation. Her previous delivery had shoulder dystocia and scans have shown this baby is above ten pounds so Dr Cunningham has decided to deliver this baby by Caesarean. All observations are normal and both women have been fasting since an early breakfast at six this morning.'

'That's great, thanks, Sally. I'll have a quick read of their notes and then I'll see if I can help out anywhere else until they're due to go Theatre.'

'No probs. Right, that's me off, then. See you tomorrow.' Sally picked up her bag and headed for the changing room.

It only took Melissa a few minutes to check the notes and then re-check both ladies' observations. She recorded them in their charts and had a quick tidy up.

Julie and Wendy had their blue theatre gowns on and paper hats in place. They were both relaxed with no concerns about going to Theatre. 'Hurry up, Melissa,' urged Julie. '*Diagnosis Murder* is about to start and we want to watch it before we go to Theatre.' Melissa laughed and finished double-checking their name bands. She knew she was safe to leave the women for the moment and could help out elsewhere.

Cooper was sitting at the midwives' station when she walked along from the post-op room. He finished writing up some notes and put them back in the trolley.

'How are you doing?'

'Since you spoke to me last night? I'm feeling fine.'

'Were you sick this morning?'

'After you phoned me at six or after you phoned me at seven?'

He gave a rueful smile. 'I take it you're trying to make a point. Am I coming on too strong?'

'You're maybe just a *little* over-protective, Coop. I'm a big girl. I've looked after myself for a long time.' She wasn't quite sure that she meant it. She had always loved having her own space and certainly her flat was tiny and couldn't accommodate two. But these last few days had been hard. She couldn't face going into the kitchen to prepare food and it would be nice if someone was there to help her. Even though she had a baby inside her, for the first time her independent streak was waning and she felt very alone.

He looked at her thoughtfully. Silence. Melissa

shifted uncomfortably on her feet. The most handsome doctor in the place. She was having his baby. And she couldn't think of a word to say to him. Great. She glanced back up at the board. One of the senior students was handling her first delivery. She would go and see if she needed any support. She headed towards the room.

'Hi, Phoebe. I'm just in to see if you need anything.'

The red-haired senior student looked up from the notes she was recording and gave her a big smile. 'Hi, Melissa, that's great, thanks. This is Louise Hendry. She's twenty-four and this is her first baby. She's thirty-nine weeks' gestation. We've confirmed rupture of her membranes. Her contractions are still quite far apart, nearly seven minutes, so she's here a little earlier than normal. Louise's husband serves with the armed forces and is away on duty at the moment and she had to drive herself in. So she didn't want to wait.'

'He's due back tomorrow. I can't believe I've gone into labour today.' Melissa could hear the anxiety in the woman's voice.

Melissa gave her a smile. 'Don't worry, this

is your first baby and things could take a while. Who knows? He might just make it in time.'

Melissa bent her head to check the notes. 'Everything looks fine, Phoebe.' Phoebe was a very conscientious student who would be a great midwife in the future. This was her second placement in the labour suite and Melissa was sure she would be more than capable of dealing with this delivery.

She looked at Louise, who was sitting comfortably on the bed. She'd changed into a hospital gown and had brought an array of magazines with her. Melissa noticed her crossed ankles and had a little prod at the flesh surrounding them. Her fingerprint seemed to leave the smallest imprint in the skin, which gradually disappeared in a few seconds. Slight oedema. Not unusual in pregnant women and definitely not unusual in a third trimester. She flicked the chart over to check the blood-pressure reading that Phoebe had recorded. Normal. Everything seemed fine. But Melissa just had the strangest feeling in the pit of her stomach.

Melissa fixed a bright smile on her face. 'How are you feeling, Louise?'

Louise gave a nervous smile. 'Okay, I guess. But I'd be better if I could get rid of this nagging headache.' She pressed her fingers to her temples. 'I was too worried to take anything but it's been there since last night.'

She frowned as Melissa came around the bed to her side. 'But it's not too bad, honestly.'

'Can you put out your hand for me and clench it into a fist?'

'What?' Louise was confused.

'Really, just try for me please.'

Within just a few seconds Louise completed the test. It took her just a little longer than normal to relax her fist again. Melissa could feel her senses buzzing. Hyperactive reflexes, oedema, headache. All signs of eclampsia. Her senses were never wrong. Eclampsia was a serious condition and relatively rare. Pre-eclampsia was more common in pregnancy but was usually picked up at antenatal checks and well controlled to allow the mother to have a healthy baby and normal delivery.

'Phoebe, would you mind collecting a specimen of urine and testing it, please?'

Phoebe looked over at her, slightly confused as everything appeared fine. 'Sure, Melissa, no problem.' She hurried out the door to collect a sterile specimen container.

Melissa turned back to Louise. 'Have you had any problems with your vision in the last few days?'

'It's been a bit strange today. It was a little fuzzy when I got up this morning, but it seemed okay when I drove to the hospital. Melissa...' Louise's face had started to twitch around her mouth. Melissa knew instantly what was about to happen. She moved quickly to Louise's side. The buzzer was at the other side of the bed. 'Cooper!' she shouted at the top of her voice. Louise took a sharp intake of breath and her whole body went rigid.

The doors within the labour suite where thick and heavy, primarily to keep out noise, but this could also prevent Melissa summoning help. Melissa knew that Cooper had just been sitting at the midwives' station opposite this room. He flung open the door just as Louise started to go into a full-blown convulsion, her legs and arms thrashing around the bed.

'Pull the alarm,' she shouted, 'and help me get her on her side.'

Cooper moved effortlessly, pulling the large red button on the wall above the bed before sliding his arms underneath Louise's convulsing body and turning her on her left side to help protect the baby by allowing good uterine blood flow. Melissa reached up, grabbed an oxygen mask from the wall and turned on the supply. Cooper helped lift Louise's head as Melissa slipped the mask over her nose and mouth to administer oxygen. It wasn't unusual for breathing to be interrupted during a seizure and it was important to try and keep the oxygen levels in the blood as high as possible, for both mother and baby.

The wail of the alarm brought the sound of thudding feet along the corridor. Phoebe appeared at the door, clutching the sterile container for the urine specimen, her face frozen with terror. 'But everything was fine...' she started to say.

'I need some help, Phoebe,' said Melissa

abruptly. Her voice and tone brought Phoebe out of her stupor and she moved rapidly to Melissa's side.

'What do you want me to do?'

Louise's whole body was jerking and twitching as Melissa and Cooper attempted to hold her safely in place. Cooper's voice was clear and steady. 'Get me some magnesium sulphate, a cannula and a one-hundred-ml infusion bag.' As chaos erupted around him Cooper was the epitome of calm. Another midwife, pulling the crash cart behind her, entered the room, closely followed by the anaesthetist, whose page was still sounding. Phoebe moved swiftly, collected the supplies that Cooper needed, and placed them in his hands. 'Set up the CTG monitor,' he murmured in her ear. 'I need to see how this baby is doing.'

Melissa pulled the suction tube from the wall. 'I think we're coming to end of the seizure,' she said as Louise's limbs started to relax and cease twitching. She glanced at her watch. She had been bent low, with her ear next to Louise's mouth, to monitor her breathing while she'd been on her side. Quickly she suctioned away the oral secretions as the anaesthetist claimed his place at the head of the bed. 'All yours, Tim,' she said quietly, as she moved out of the way to allow him to take up position.

She released the brake from the bottom of the bed and pulled the bed sharply out from its place at the wall. Tim would need room to do his assessment. She turned on the cardiac monitor and set up the leads, blood-pressure cuff and slid the pulse oximeter onto one of Louise's fingers. As Phoebe started the CTG trace Melissa quickly checked the leads and monitored the reading as it came out. 'Oxygen saturation is ninety-two per cent and blood pressure has just spiked,' she called to Tim, who gave her a swift nod.

Melissa worked her way around to the other side of the bed. 'Seizure lasted forty-five seconds,' she said to Cooper, who had drawn up the drug to prevent subsequent seizures and had started to slowly administer it.

Melissa looked at the IV bag sitting on the locker top. 'Do you want me to set up the continuous infusion for once you're finished with the loading dose?'

Cooper nodded, watching the clock on the nearby wall as he continued with the medicine. The loading dose had to be delivered slowly, over fifteen to twenty minutes. Melissa grabbed an IV giving set and pump. 'One gram an hour?' she double-checked with Cooper, before priming the pump and setting it to run. 'It's ready whenever you're finished.'

She made to turn and head back to other side of the room but Cooper grabbed her hand. 'Are you okay? Did you get kicked?'

'No, Cooper, I'm fine.'

'It was a good call, Melissa. I'm impressed.'

She was bewildered. She'd only shouted for him when the facial twitching had started. 'What do you mean?'

'You knew something was wrong, didn't you?'

She gave a little nod.

'Phoebe had stopped to speak to me outside. She told me you'd asked her to collect a urine specimen. And that you'd checked for oedema, hyperactive reflexes and a headache.' He glanced over to where Phoebe was recording Louise's latest readings. 'She wondered what made you suspect something was wrong.'

Melissa shrugged her shoulders. 'Initially it was just a hunch.' She smiled at his furrowed brow. 'I noticed the smallest amount of oedema in her legs. Her blood-pressure recording was entirely normal but I just got the strangest feeling. Once I'd established she had some other symptoms I just knew. But I didn't expect her to start seizing so quickly.'

He gave a thoughtful little nod. 'I was supposed to be heading to the clinic but when Phoebe started to speak to me I decided to hang around a little longer.' He shot her a glance. 'I was waiting to see if the urine specimen was positive for protein. I knew you would call me for a consult.' He stopped for a second, giving her a little smile. 'You've got good instincts, Missy.'

The words sent a warm feeling spreading through her. It was nice to know that he respected her professionally—even if she didn't really know how he felt about her.

He glanced over at Tim, who had signalled that

Louise had started to come round. It was unlikely she would remember anything that had just happened. 'I'm going to consult with Tim about what we do next. We need to get this baby out soon.'

Melissa gave a nod of her head and moved away, grabbing the midwifery notes and taking another look at the CTG monitor. 'Baby's heart rate is a little slow, just as we'd expect after a seizure.'

She looked over at Phoebe. The student midwife was monitoring the baby's heart rate meticulously but her hands were trembling. Jen, one of the other midwives, had entered the room and followed Melissa's gaze. She put her hand on Melissa's shoulder and gave her an almost imperceptible nod. It wasn't uncommon for staff members to need some time out after a traumatic event, particularly if they were students. 'I'm just going to take Phoebe away for ten minutes for a debrief,' Melissa said as she stood up and placed her hand over Phoebe's. 'Jen will take over while we go and get a quick cup of tea.'

Phoebe nodded gratefully as Jen stepped up behind her to take her place.

Melissa headed over to the door then took a deep breath as she felt a pair of hands behind her, grasping her waist.

Cooper spoke in a low, husky voice. 'Are you sure you're okay?'

Melissa nodded wordlessly, aware of their close proximity in the tightly packed room.

'Good,' he said swiftly as he leaned over and his lips brushed the side of her cheek with a casualness as if he did it every day, in full view of everyone in the room.

Melissa's fingers flew to the spot on her cheek where he'd just kissed her. She was stunned. She knew she should be angry but as she left the room she could feel a warm glow spreading through her. Cooper was worried about her. He was worried about her and the baby. Maybe she wasn't as alone as she'd thought she was.

'Melissa!'

Cooper banged on the door for the third time and waited—still no response.

He glanced at his watch. It was nearly eight o'clock and Melissa should have reported for duty an hour ago. Andrea, one of the ward sisters, had phoned him to say Melissa hadn't appeared and wasn't answering her mobile or her home phone, something she would never do. Cooper had raced over to Missy's flat and had been able to duck inside the main doorway as another resident was leaving. But now he was left in the hallway with no sign of Melissa.

He glanced over his shoulders at the two facing doors. No one was at home in either of those flats, he'd already tried their doors. Biting his lip, he knelt down and prised open Melissa's letter box. Thankfully she hadn't opted for one of those 'bolt outside' mailboxes. It was dark in the hallway of Melissa's flat with a little light gleaming at the end of the hall coming from Melissa's living room. He inched over on his knees to try and get a better view. He thought he could see something…

Yes, there it was. A pair of feet. But not lying on the floor. Was she sitting on the sofa? Cooper pulled back from the letterbox. Why on earth would she be sitting on the sofa while he was bellowing at the door?

His heart sank when he realised something else. She still had her slippers on her feet—bright red fluffy slippers—not the flat, white work shoes she normally wore. And he knew immediately why she hadn't got that far.

He pulled his phone from his pocket to call the emergency services then shook his head. He glanced around him once more to make sure no one had sneaked up on him while he'd been peering through her door, but there was no one else there. No one else to help him.

And he wasn't going to wait. Who knew how long it would take an ambulance to get there? Then they would need the police to break down her door. No, this was the mother of his child and something was very wrong. Time was of the essence and there was no way Cooper could stand here, waiting for the police and ambulance to arrive, while Melissa was in there unwell.

He stepped back, lifted his foot and with all his strength…

The noise was phenomenal. Like a car ramming into a brick wall. Splintered wood flew all around as the door lay in pieces before him. For a second he hesitated, expecting people to appear shouting all around him. But there was nothing.

Cooper stepped over the fractured pieces of wood and in three long strides was in her living room. His breath caught in his throat.

He'd never seen Melissa look like this before. She was sitting on the sofa in a tiny red satin nightdress with her huge slippers on her feet. Her skin was pale and washed out with tiny beads of sweat glistening on her brow. She had a glazed expression on her face, as if she was contemplating something really complicated, but her eyes remained blank. As if she was vacant, as if she was not really there. She hadn't even noticed him come into the room. More worryingly, she hadn't even reacted to the noise.

He'd never seen Melissa have a hypoglycaemic attack before. Every diabetic was an individual and had different signs and symptoms of an oncoming attack. But he had absolutely no doubt what was wrong with her. He had to get some kind of sugar into her, and fast.

He knelt down in front of her and grabbed her shoulders, flinching at how cold they were.

'Missy, Melissa, it's Cooper. Melissa, can you speak?'

Melissa's head was spinning. She knew something wasn't right, but she wasn't quite sure what it was. She felt as if she were in a dream. She was aware of lights flickering around her and of some noise in the background, but she didn't know what it was. And she was cold, so cold. She knew she should get up and put her housecoat on but her legs just felt so heavy. She would do it in a minute. Yes, that's what she'd do.

Cooper looked frantically around the flat. She didn't look in any fit state to eat, she looked as if she was barely conscious. He took a deep breath. Melissa was the most organised woman he knew. Glucagon. She would have glucagon somewhere. It was the glucose injection that doctors and paramedics gave to diabetic patients who had lost consciousness. It gave a sharp boost of glucose to the system, which generally brought the patient round.

He went into the kitchen and pulled open the fridge. There it was, the tell-tale orange box, in the shelf on the door next to her insulin. He yanked out one of the ready-made syringes and injected the water into the glucose powder solution, gave it a quick shake and withdrew the mixture again.

He stood at the doorway, contemplating for a second the best place to inject her, before lifting her slip and pushing the needle into her thigh. It would take too long to find a viable vein, she was too cold and too shut down. Intramuscular injection would take a few extra minutes to work but that was fine, he had all the time in the world.

He walked into her bedroom, barely even taking in the surroundings before grabbing her duvet from the bed, bringing it through to the living room and wrapping it around her. He took a few seconds to switch on the kettle and rummaged through the cupboards to find some teabags and sugar, obviously hardly ever used, in the cupboard. As soon as she was conscious he had to get some sugar into her.

Cooper sat back down on the sofa next to Melissa. He wrapped one arm around her shoulder and pulled her closer, his other arm on her leg, rubbing the injection site in the hope it would hasten the effects of the jag.

This was going to be the longest five minutes of his life.

Ouch! Melissa's head hurt and so did her leg. What had happened? She tried to make sense of her surroundings. Where was she? Her mouth felt dry and she was desperate for something to drink. Her eyes gradually focused. Cooper was sitting next to her on the sofa and she had her red duvet wrapped around her, but she was so cold. What on earth had happened? And what on earth was Cooper doing there? This didn't look good.

Her hand flew to her stomach. Was the baby okay?

Cooper's hand was on her leg. He was watching her closely. 'You had a hypo,' he said.

'What?' Her brain was slowly starting to work again. 'But my blood-sugar level was fine.'

'No, it wasn't,' Cooper said quietly. 'I checked it while you were passed out, it was way below normal.'

'Oh.' She caught sight of the tell-tale orange

box that lay opened on the nearby table. That must be why her leg was hurting and why Cooper's hand was rubbing her thigh. He had injected her.

'I'm supposed to be at work.' She groaned and leaned back on the sofa. 'How did you get in here, Cooper? How did you even know I wasn't well?'

Cooper gave an apologetic smile. 'Andrea phoned me when you didn't report for duty. As for how I got in here....' His eyes glanced down the corridor towards the shattered door. 'We're going to have to discuss that. You really need to improve your security in this flat.'

Melissa gave half a smile. She still felt a little fuzzy.

Cooper stood up. 'Give me a second. I'm going to make you some toast and tea.'

He returned a few minutes later with two steaming cups of tea and pile of buttered toast, which he placed on the table in front of them.

Melissa lifted a cup and took a sip. 'Yuck! That tastes awful!'

He smiled. 'That's the taste of real sugar. Now, drink it, lady, whether you like it or not. Doctor's orders.' He winked at her. She was finally coming back to normal. He'd never felt so relieved. He watched for a few minutes as she ate her toast and drank her tea. He'd finally managed to take his hand from her thigh but, truth be told, his hand still tingled. In the heat of the moment he hadn't had time to admire Melissa in her short red satin nightdress. But, now as they sat companionably on the sofa, he could. Her breasts were definitely fuller than he remembered, more rounded in appearance and barely hidden behind the thin material and spaghetti straps. And then there had been the other discovery as he'd pushed the nightdress aside to administer the injection— Melissa didn't wear any panties under that nightie.

He'd averted his eyes from the tiny dark triangle of curls, because it had been the last thing on his mind, but now...

Melissa moved in his arms, turning around to face him and bringing his mind first and foremost to the present situation.

'What time is it, Cooper? You said that Andrea had phoned you. Am I late?'

He shook his head. 'Forget about work, Missy. Right now that's not important.'

'I'm really sorry about this, and I'm so embarrassed.' She gestured to her nightdress and slippers. 'I've no idea what state you found me in this morning. I'd obviously got up to get ready for work and I've no idea what happened after that. This just isn't like me.'

Cooper took in her serious expression with sympathy—she was definitely back to normal now. 'You know this can happen in pregnancy, Melissa. It doesn't matter how well controlled your diabetes has been in the past. This is a whole different ball game. Being pregnant can make your blood-sugar levels drop a lot quicker than normal. You've helped out at the diabetic antenatal clinic. You know that this happens to some of the women.'

Melissa gave a big sigh. 'But I didn't expect it to happen to me. I didn't get the warning signs that I normally get—the ones that give me enough time to go and eat something.' She threw her hands in the air in exasperation. 'I'm always in complete control. How am I supposed to figure this out?'

Alarm bells started going off in Cooper's head. There was something not right about her reaction to this. 'This has happened before, hasn't it?'

Her face as white as snow, she mumbled a response.

'What?'

He felt worried, irritated even, but now was not the time for that kind of response. He took her hand in his, noticing her skin was finally beginning to warm up again. 'Now, tell me, has this happened before?'

She sighed and ran her fingers through her unruly curls. 'A few times.'

'As bad as this?'

'No, no, of course not. I've always managed to eat something before it got too bad, well, almost always…'

'Melissa?' Cooper's brown eyes were filled with concern. 'What do you mean, "almost always"?'

'I've had a few near misses at night. I've been setting my alarm so I get up in the middle of the night and have something to eat.'

Cooper could feel his breath catch at the back of

his throat. Why hadn't he seen any of this? Why hadn't she told him? He'd been speaking to her every day—sometimes three times a day—and she hadn't said a word. She needed help. Fast. And it was his job to give it. Her independent streak was putting her and their baby at risk. He looked at his surroundings, flinching as he remembered what he'd done to her door. 'You need to come and stay with me. It's not safe, for you or the baby.'

Melissa was horrified. 'No! I can't. I'll be fine—this is just a little blip. I've always managed my diabetes and I'll manage this too.'

Cooper shook his head. He was not taking no for an answer. He'd seen the state she'd been in that morning and he couldn't ever let that happen again. 'I would never forgive myself if something happened to you or the baby.'

Melissa felt as if the world was closing in on her. She tried to process the words he'd just said. *You or the baby*. Did that mean he felt something for her too? Or was this only just about the baby?

Her head was spinning. No matter how hard she tried to stop it, Cooper was getting well and truly under her skin. She'd started to find herself waiting for his texts and calls, and loving it when they finally came. But this was a man who was still grieving for his wife so she couldn't allow herself to become emotionally attached to him, not when he couldn't feel the same way about her. She'd seen what hurt like that did to a woman.

'Stop it. Leave me alone.' The tears were welling up in her eyes and before she knew it, they were spilling down her cheeks. 'I'm not giving up my independence for anyone. I love staying in my own flat. You can phone me, text me or come and visit, but I'm not going to stay with you.' She tried to sound determined.

Cooper put his arm around her. 'But I have been phoning you, Missy, and you haven't told me a thing. No one is asking you to give up your independence. You're right. This is only a blip. It might only last a few weeks but you still need some help. What if you had a really bad hypo during the night? Who could inject you to bring you round? If you were on duty the next day someone would notice when you didn't appear. But what if you weren't on duty? What if you were on days off? You could lie unconscious for three days before anyone came looking for you. I can't let that happen.'

The words cut through Melissa like a knife. The thought chilled her to the bone. She couldn't let that happen either. Her baby's safety was paramount. 'You could phone me every day, at the same time, and if I didn't answer—'

'Not good enough.' Cooper cut her off briskly. 'Like I said, I've been phoning you every day for the last three weeks but it obviously isn't enough. It would be better if we were under one roof. That way, I might realise when you were about to have a hypo and do something to stop it.'

Melissa shook her head. She knew he was right. She had always been able to tell when her blood-sugar levels were low. Sometimes she would break out in a sweat, other times she would tremble. Sometimes she just had the strangest feeling in the pit of her stomach. But now it was different. Her warning signs had changed, they were much more subtle, and she wasn't picking up on them.

Melissa stared blankly into space. This was

turning into the worst day of her life. Could she separate her heart from her head? Could she stay with Cooper for a few weeks until her hypos were under control, without losing her heart completely?

Cooper gave her one of his winning smiles. The kind that was seen on an advertising billboard for toothpaste. 'Missy, I would offer to come and stay with you but we need to have a little chat about that. And about getting your door fixed.'

Her eyebrows lifted. She hadn't moved from this sofa since she'd had the hypo and she'd wondered how on earth Cooper had gotten into her flat. Now she knew.

Melissa took a deep breath. She felt as if this decision could cause her physical pain. Her heart was screaming *No* but her head was screaming *Yes*! It went against all her principles. But she didn't just have herself to think about any more. She had to put the baby first and this was the most obvious solution. 'Okay, Cooper, I'll come and stay with you. But only on a temporary basis. Once this blip has passed I'll be moving back to my own flat, okay?'

Cooper nodded. Right now he would agree to anything. He needed to keep both her and the baby safe.

'And you're definitely getting me a new front door, right?'

He smiled and drew her into his arms, planting a kiss on her forehead. 'Everything's going to be okay, Missy.'

She sat for a few seconds, enjoying the waves of warmth that swept from his body to hers. She and Cooper alone together at last. Even the thought of it sent other types of waves running through her body causing her nipples to instantly prickle to attention. She shifted uncomfortably. She could try this. She had to try this, because she had to know. She had to know if she could be in a room with Cooper and stop thinking about him in ways that didn't involve him wearing no clothes. She had to know that she could become immune to those big brown eyes and killer smiles. She had to know that she could have a civilised relationship with the father of her child.

Melissa stood up. The side effects of the glucose injection were starting to kick in. On the few occasions she'd ever been given it she'd always been violently sick. The tell-tale waves of nausea began to sweep across her. She gave Cooper a weak smile. 'You might just live to regret this, Coop.'

CHAPTER SEVEN

COOPER stirred the pot for the nineteenth time and tried to stop the chicken sticking to the bottom of the pan. He wasn't too good at this but he was determined to try. The stainless-steel kitchen currently looked like a disaster zone. There were three pans in the kitchen sink, every worktop space was filled with ingredients and utensils, and the cookery book he'd propped against a wall kept sliding downwards and automatically closing. To top it all off, everything was covered in a thin coating of flour following an incident with a dropped bag. But no matter how much chaos ensued, above all Cooper was feeling happy.

After a week of sharing a home and cobbling meals together from the remnants of Cooper's freezer they'd finally gone shopping. That morning he'd learned that Melissa loved chicken, hated beef, was funny about fish and absolutely detested prawns. Just as well in her current condition. He knew she loved chocolate, but limited her supply to the occasional square and she seemed to drink gallons of a diet brand of drink from Scotland. And she had a penchant for beans on toast, late at night.

'Can I give you a hand in there?' called Melissa. She was currently lying across the red sofa, reading the latest bestseller. She could vaguely see the disarray surrounding Cooper, but she was having too much fun watching him trying to cook her dinner to go and help.

'No,' shouted Cooper. 'I've told you, just relax.' He stirred frantically as the chicken seemed to stick to the bottom of the pan for the twentieth time that evening. His rice boiled over with huge hissing sounds as the water hit the steel hob. He looked at the slightly overdone chicken and the definitely overdone rice, before heaving a sigh and turning off the gas hob. It would have to do.

He found a tray that he'd never known he owned and stuck the two plates on it to carry through to the living room. From a plastic bag hidden behind the microwave he found his secret purchase from that afternoon and put it next to her plate.

'Here we go.' Cooper plunked the tray down on the coffee table next to Melissa as she swung her legs off the sofa. He watched her as she gazed in amazement at the gift and a smile spread across her face. She leaned over and picked it up.

The little ultrasound picture had been placed in a red frame to match the décor in the room. 'You put it in a frame?' she asked, momentarily stunned.

'I thought it should have pride of place,' he said, leaning next to her to look at the picture. 'I also thought we could probably update it every four weeks when you get your new scans.'

The smile reached up to her ears. 'That's a nice thought,' she whispered quietly. She turned to face him and he automatically clasped his arms around her waist, pulling her close. 'Why did you do that?' she asked.

He ran his finger down her cheek. 'I knew that you'd been upset with me in the scan room. I also knew how big a deal it was for you to come and live here. I wanted you both to feel welcome.'

Melissa felt the warm feeling inside her begin to spread. Cooper had said *both. He wanted both of them to feel welcome.* Something about this just felt so right. Today had been a great day. She'd been relaxed and happy in his company. He'd been attentive without being overbearing. He'd massaged her shoulders when they'd come back from town and had made her tea.

She'd enjoyed going shopping with him, even though he was the most disorganised shopper she'd ever met. Now she understood why he piled food onto his plate in the hospital canteen as if it was going out of fashion. It was because he never ate at home. He didn't see the point in cooking for one. Her heart had almost melted when he'd said those words.

She'd reorganised his trolley with dinners for every night of the week for both of them and numerous snacks. She'd bought the biggest range of breakfast cereals, along with eggs, bacon and orange juice. 'Do not let me leave the house in the morning without breakfast,' she'd warned him, and he'd nodded dutifully and paid the huge grocery bill without a flicker of surprise.

Melissa had caught sight of them both in one of the large mirrors in the supermarket as they'd shopped. They had looked like any other couple, laughing and joking their way around the shop while he'd put things in the trolley and she'd taken them back out with a shake of her head. She'd felt a pang in her heart. This was only temporary. They hadn't had that discussion about the future yet. There was still so much she was unsure of. But the fact that he had put their baby's ultrasound picture in a frame was a good start.

She stared down at the congealing chicken on the plate before her and stifled a laugh. 'Are all your dinners going to be as good as this one?'

He nodded enthusiastically at her. 'I've spent hours over that. I expect you to clean your plate.'

Melissa gulped and made to lift the fork in front of her.

'We need to talk about something.'

'Sure. What is it?' Anything that stopped her from eating this dinner.

'What do you want to do about work? After you have the baby, I mean.'

Melissa looked him, a little surprised at where

the conversation had gone, but she knew it was time for them to talk about this. 'I think that I'd like to take my whole years' maternity leave and then go back to work.' She wondered if Cooper would object. Would he expect her to be a full-time mum?

But Cooper nodded thoughtfully. 'Do you still plan on working full time or will you reduce your hours?'

'I'd like to do fewer hours, it all depends on how things work out financially. In an ideal world I'd do two days and spend the rest of the time at home with the baby.'

His brown eyes were studying her carefully. 'You know that I'll support you, don't you? Financially and in real terms.' He went to continue but Melissa had already interrupted.

'I don't want your money, Cooper.'

He raised his hand. 'But the money isn't for *you*, Melissa, it's for our *baby*.' He raised his eyebrow at her defensive tone. 'You know this independent streak of yours runs a mile wide, but isn't always in your own best interests. Every man on the planet should support their child and that's what I intend to do. And if that helps you reduce the number of hours that you work, that's fine.'

She shifted uncomfortably. She hated talking about money. It was inevitable that they would have this conversation but it just didn't feel right. The reality was that child support from Cooper probably would allow her to reduce her working hours, but the thought of being dependent on someone else for something like that was alien to her.

'I just learned from an early age not to be dependent on a man.'

Cooper's eyes looked up at the quiet tone of her voice. 'How did you learn that, Missy?'

Her fingers went automatically to her hair, just as they always did when she was uncomfortable, and she started twisting a chestnut lock. 'My dad left when I was eleven. My mum had always thought the world revolved around him, she was devastated and fell apart. I was left to pick up the pieces.'

Cooper could feel the hair on his arms stand on end. This was the first time Missy had really shared something so important with him. 'That sounds tough. Do you still see him?'

'Not since the day he walked out. He left us for another woman. He sent me a few letters and cards, some money for birthdays, but it would have been too difficult on my mum if I'd tried to see him.'

Cooper felt annoyed. An eleven-year-old child shouldn't have to make a decision like that. 'Did he try to see you?'

She nodded. 'Yes, a few times. But it never worked out. On the days I had arranged to meet him, Mum always had one crisis or another.'

His hand reached out and encircled hers. 'But you were a child, you shouldn't have had to deal with that.'

'But I did. There was no one else. My mum was clinically depressed for a long time. We had to sell our house and move. She'd never had a job before and it took a long time before she was ready to go out and look for work.'

'And now?'

'She's doing well. She lives in her own flat and works in the local library. She just about manages her finances. I help her out occasionally. Her mental health is much better. But I never want to end up like her, end up in a state like that over a man.'

The words hung between them. Cooper was processing everything she'd just said. Now he understood her actions. Now he understood her independent streak. Missy took a deep breath. Cooper wasn't her father. And he wasn't David either. But she wasn't ready to agree to anything yet. There was still too much that could change between them.

'I'll wait until nearer the time,' she said quickly. 'I'll decide what I want to do then.' She bent her head over her dinner, to escape his watchful eyes.

'But what about Junior?'

'What about Junior?' The first mouthful of Cooper's chicken had just made it into her mouth. She wasn't altogether keen to try another.

'I'm not just talking about money here, Melissa. I want to be involved in our baby's life. All the time if I can.' He made a sweeping gesture with his arm. 'You know that I've got plenty of space here. If you were working at the week-end and I wasn't on call, I'd be happy to have Junior. During the day and overnight.'

Wow. Her baby staying somewhere else overnight. She hadn't even thought about that yet.

'And I could look at my shifts during the week too if that would help.'

Missy nodded, taking a deep breath. 'I had planned on using the hospital crèche if I had to. But if you could help out, that would be good too.' Her voice was hesitant. As if this was the first time she'd really given it any proper thought and the processes were just forming in her mind.

'I want to be here to help you and the baby.'

She turned to face him as he reached over and touched her arm. There it was again, that delicious zing that appeared out of nowhere whenever he touched her. She had just gone to lift a second mouthful of chicken to her lips but Cooper hadn't let her go yet. He was staring deeply into her eyes. 'I need to talk to you about something else.'

She sat the fork back down, noting the serious expression on his face. Her stomach clenched. *What was he going to say now?*

Cooper leaned forward, staring at her with

those big chocolate eyes of his. 'I haven't slept a wink since you moved in here.'

She was confused. Why was he telling her this now? 'Why on earth can't you sleep?'

'I can't sleep because I'm constantly worrying that you could be having a hypo in the other room.'

'Oh.' She nodded her head slowly. 'And?'

A slow smile crept across his lips. 'I was thinking that it might make more sense if we slept in the same bed.'

'I see.' She breathed in slowly, her brain screaming one answer while her heart thudded another. She finally felt as if a weight had been lifted off her shoulders. Maybe Cooper would understand why she felt so strongly about things now? Maybe that could leave them free to concentrate on other things?

'If you were unwell during the night, I wouldn't realise until the next morning. If you were lying next to me, I would be much more likely to notice sooner.' Cooper gave her a lazy smile before moving closer and running a finger along the base of her neck. Missy felt her heartbeat quicken. Her breath caught in her lungs.

'So you want me to sleep in the white bedroom, then?'

Cooper raised his eyes from her neck and nodded slowly. 'What do you think?' He held his breath while he waited for her answer.

Missy looked at the plate of unappetising food on the table to her side. She could think of much better things to eat. This man was haunting her every waking thought. Part of her wondered if sleeping with Cooper again could get him finally out of her system. These pregnancy hormones were playing havoc with her senses, and it was all she could do not to pin him up against the wall. Other parts wondered if she was just trying to hold onto whatever little bit of him she could get. It was time to find out.

'Will there be any special treatment if I decide to sleep in the white room with you?'

Cooper's face relaxed. He knew where this was heading. 'I can think of some.'

Missy stood up and took his hand. 'Well, in that case I think I'll have a demonstration.'

She took him by the hand and led him across the living room, pushing open the door to his bedroom and stepping onto the thick white carpet. Her toes automatically curled in pleasure at the deep-piled carpet, reminding her of the last time she'd been in this room. Had that really been nearly five months ago?

She paused, turning to face him. It was dark outside, the lights from the flickering marina, reflecting on the black surface of the water like glistening stars, casting shadows into the dark bedroom. She shrugged off her thick cardigan, leaving it to puddle on the floor at her feet. She didn't want anything between them now. He lifted his hands and cupped her face, bending to kiss her. Missy's head started to spin. She'd just been about to say something, just been about to ask him if he was sure. But her words were lost as his lips touched hers, taking her back in time to a few months before.

Everything about this felt so right. They'd finally managed to have a conversation about 'their' child. To plan for the future. To look at practicalities. Maybe she could rely on Cooper?

Her body responded instantly to him, the fine hairs on her arms standing on end at the touch of his skin against hers. His hands dropped, and the slightest of stubble on his chin scraped against her face. His hands circled her waist and he walked her backwards, lowering her gently against the deep white duvet.

'Okay?' One word. It was all he said, his voice deep and husky with desire. She nodded. Nothing else mattered right now. The thousand words that needed to be said had vanished from her mind. He traced a finger from her shoulder, along the inside of her arm to the palm of her hand. She automatically closed her fingers around it, trapping it next to her, before raising her hand to her breast and releasing it there. This was what she wanted. She wanted him to touch her again, to make her feel the way he had that first magical night together. Could she ever recapture that?

His lips bent to her neck and she let out a moan. It was obvious he remembered the most sensitive part of her neck. The part that always distracted her and spun her into a new reality. A reality where she lived as a princess in a castle and this was her prince, the man who loved and adored her, and would stay with her forever. Where had that come from? Yup, she was definitely losing her mind.

She felt the tug of his hand at her jeans and automatically went to pull her stomach in, then realised that she couldn't. A remnant of their last night of passion. The last time she'd been in this bedroom.

He quickly removed her clothes, pulling her jeans from her legs and sliding her top from her shoulders. She sighed as he ran his hand slowly down the inside of her thigh, then back up again.

Missy tugged at his shirt, desperate to feel his skin against hers. The hairs on his chest brushed against her face as he pulled his shirt over his head.

She could practically feel the electricity sparking between them. She ran her fingers over his warm skin, pulling him even closer to her. .

She lifted her head, whispering in his ear, 'Why are we waiting, Coop?' A smile danced across her lips as she teased him. 'It's not like we need to worry about contraception.'

He was poised above her now, his arms on either side of her shoulders. There was a gleam in his deep brown eyes. 'I guess we don't,' he said huskily. His head bent downwards and she gasped as his tongue ran down her throat towards her nipple. He nudged her bra aside and teased her with his teeth.

'You're driving me crazy, Cooper,' she moaned, before catching his buttocks with the palms of her hands and driving him towards her. There, she could definitely feel him now. And she knew exactly what she wanted.

'No more teasing.' Her voice was low as she lifted her hips from the bed and moved herself against him. He lifted his head, his breathing hoarse. 'I hope you're sure, Missy.'

'I'm sure.'

His hand swept aside her silk panties, removing the final barrier between them. She heard a guttural moan in response before he thrust into her, filling her completely, then smiled and pulled backwards.

The sensations started seeping through Melissa. This was what she remembered. This was what she wanted. He was taunting her, teasing her. Her legs wrapped instinctively around him, keeping him close, her hands around his neck as his head dipped lower towards her sensitive nipples.

'Cooper,' she moaned. 'Don't stop.'

The pulses were growing stronger, her breath catching in her throat. She moved her hips in synch with his, lifting them off the bed to pull him deeper inside her.

'Missy,' he growled as his rhythm grew faster.

And she was lost. Nothing had felt this good. Nothing *could* feel this good. Only him.

Cooper woke just as the first rays of early morning sunshine streamed through the window. For a second he forgot where he was, encompassed by warmth, bare skin against bare skin, his arm wrapped around Missy's waist, the palm of his hand resting on her blossoming stomach. His eyes flickered open as her hair tickled his nose. Chestnut-brown hair.

He started, pulling back from Missy's warm body. His breath caught in his throat. He groaned, reality striking him like a hammer blow. Blonde. He had expected to see blonde hair.

Just for a second, when he'd been in that dream-like state between sleep and wakening, he'd been transported back in time. Back to a past where everything had been fine and he'd had hopes and expectations for the future. He gave an involuntary shudder. This had happened before. For the first few days after Clara and Lily had died, when he'd woken in the morning, for a second—just for a second—everything had been fine. Then, like an avalanche of tumbling rocks, it had hit him all again. The horror. The loss. The desperation.

He knew that this was normal. That anyone who had suffered a bereavement went through these feelings. But this wasn't Clara. He was lying in bed with another woman. Another woman who was carrying his child. Cooper pulled back. Last time he'd slept with Missy she'd disappeared before morning. He woken up to an empty bed, and he'd been disappointed. His eyes swept over her sleeping form. His hand still rested on her stomach. The first signs of gentle blooming were present and he felt numb. Everything was topsy-turvy between them and that said nothing about his feelings. Not because he wasn't happy about being a father, simply because he was numb with fear. But, just like last night, put him in an enclosed space with Melissa and all sense went out of the window and his raging hormones took over.

With every day that passed he was witnessing Missy's body bloom swell with his child. He would soon see the first little kicks and squirms of the life within. And no matter how hard he tried, he just couldn't feel joy. He'd seen the look on her face in the scan room; he'd seen the same wonder and awe on the faces of many parents at that first sight of their baby. But something had happened deep inside him. His heart felt as if it were wrapped in a layer of ice. He had to protect himself. He wanted to be a father. He wanted to have the happy life that he'd seen the family down at the marina having. He wanted to be excited and whip out the scan picture of his baby to show anyone who asked. But the fear wouldn't leave him. He'd done all these things the first time—the joy, the happiness, the plans.

In a couple of weeks they would be going for their detailed scan. The scan that would show their baby's development. *Please let everything be fine*. He sent a silent prayer upwards. Fear crept down his spine. The thought of packing up another nursery into boxes made him feel physically sick. Putting the tiny white and yellow vests and sleepsuits into a box had almost killed him. Phoning the shop to tell them he wouldn't be picking up the pram and hearing the sob at the back of the unknown woman's throat had been too much.

Packing away the cot had been the worst day of his life. It had finalised his grief. It had made him realise that it wasn't a bad dream and he wasn't going to wake up in the morning and find out that everything was all right. It had made him realise Clara and Lily were gone forever. It had almost been the undoing of him.

And now, two years on, he found himself in this position, an unplanned baby with a woman who had a long-term medical condition. A condition that meant she and the baby were at higher risk of everything, every complication his imagination could throw at him—and right now his mind was working overtime.

He couldn't deny the attraction he felt towards Missy. She was magnetic. He'd caught sight of her numerous times at work when she'd been dealing with patients and seen the compassion in her eyes. He felt her presence as soon as she walked into the same room as him. He just couldn't stay away from her. But this?

His rational and methodical brain told him that after his previous experience he would never have chosen to start a family with Missy. She was just too high risk. Because of his medical background, everyone would expect him to be understanding of her condition, and he was. But everyone didn't know about his past experience. And that was with someone who had been apparently healthy. He just didn't know if his heart and brain could cope with the possibility of a loss again.

Which left him here, in this position, where he wanted to reach out and be happy but his heart wouldn't let him.

He wasn't even entirely sure how he felt about

her. Did he love her? Did he even know what love was any more?

She had certainly gotten under his skin. But more than that, more than physical attraction, he liked her. He enjoyed being in her company, he loved how she was so passionate about her job. He had no doubt in the world that Missy would be a great mum. But if things went well for her and the baby, would she want to have a life with him? Would she even want to see him? Would she want him to be father to their child?

All these things were spinning around in Cooper's head and now, because he was worried about her and the baby, she was under his roof. He would see her every day. He would no longer have time to himself, to sit at night, stare out at the marina and sort out his thoughts from the day.

She looked so happy, so peaceful, even in her sleep. But his stomach was twisting. He shouldn't be here. Because, right or wrong, this felt like a betrayal. He needed some distance. He pulled back. Missy gave a sigh at his movement and turned towards him, seeking out the heat within the bed.

Cooper sat up abruptly, swinging his legs out of the bed. He took a few steps, pulling open a drawer and tugging on a pair of jogging bottoms before striding through to the kitchen. His fingers tugged at the handle on the door before he slowed his actions and quietly closed the door behind him. There was no point in making too much noise, he didn't want to wake Missy. He didn't want to have to face the consequences of what he'd done last night. He didn't want to have the inevitable conversation. What he needed right now was space.

Missy arched her back and gave a comfortable sigh. She stretched out like a cat, spreading her arms under the duvet. Space. Something wasn't right.

Her eyelids fluttered open, her hand lying in the wide open space next to her. And it was cold. There was no comfortable 'dip' in the mattress next to her. Cooper hadn't just got up to go to the toilet, he'd been gone some time.

Missy sat up, suddenly conscious of her nakedness, pulling the cover up to her chin. Where was he?

The sun was flooding through the exposed window, revealing the boats bobbing in the marina. She bit her lip. In their haste to reach the bed last night they hadn't even managed to pull the curtains. Colour flooded her cheeks as she saw her clothes scattered across the bedroom floor and she felt confusion build in her chest. Where was he? Why hadn't she woken up next to him?

The scattered clothes conjured up pictures in her mind of the heat between them last night. She didn't even want to shrug her way back into them. Her eyes caught sight of Cooper's navy fleece dressing gown hanging on a hook on the back of the bedroom door. That would do.

She opened the door and was hit by the strong aroma of coffee. As if it had been percolating for hours. Cooper cut a lonely figure, standing at the window, staring out over the marina. There was no steam rising from the mug of coffee in his hand. Probably long-cold. How long had he been standing there?

'Cooper?'

She started towards him, a tight feeling in her chest.

He flinched at her voice then turned towards her. 'Oh, you're awake.' His voice was flat, almost detached. He placed his coffee mug on the table. 'Are you hungry? Do you want me to make you breakfast?' He moved past her, almost as if she wasn't there, his eyes not making contact with hers.

Missy watched as he pulled some bread from a paper wrapper and slotted it into the toaster. He moved as if on autopilot, switching on the kettle, pulling plates from the cupboard and butter from the fridge. Never once looking at her. No friendly smile. No good-morning kiss.

A feeling of dread swept over her. She swallowed, her throat dry and parched, suddenly conscious of the ache between her legs from last night.

'Cooper.'

Nothing. Not even a flicker from him. It was as if she hadn't spoken.

She moved round behind the breakfast bar. 'Cooper.' Her voice was firmer, more definite and she laid her hand over his.

He flinched visibly. Then furiously started buttering toast.

'Cooper, what's wrong?'

'Nothing. Nothing's wrong.' He still hadn't looked at her.

'The hell it isn't!' She took the knife from his hand and put her hands on his shoulders, turning him to face her. 'Look at me, Cooper.'

She saw him bite his bottom lip, his eyes fixed firmly to the floor.

She gritted her teeth. 'I said look at me, Cooper.'

He shook his head and turned his attention to the kettle, pouring boiling water into two mugs.

She slammed her hand down on the counter next to him. 'Enough!'

That got his attention. He raised his eyebrow at her—as he had on so many other occasions—but the expression on his face wasn't amusement or annoyance. He looked exhausted. 'Leave it, Missy.'

'No, I won't leave it, Cooper. Is this it? I do this...' She swept her arms around the room. 'I agree to move in, just like you asked me to, we start to get to know each other a little better—maybe even start to have some kind of relationship—then we sleep together, and suddenly that's it? You shut me out?'

He hadn't moved. His eyes were fixed on hers. She saw him swallowing uncomfortably, as if her words were sticking in his throat.

She reached out and grabbed his arm. 'Why are you making me feel as if we did something wrong? Because I don't think we did, Cooper. I thought we did something beautiful. I thought we were two single, consenting adults. So why are you making me feel like this?'

His words seemed to falter. 'It's just...' He stared back out over the marina. 'It's difficult. It's harder than I thought.'

Missy felt a wave of nausea sweep over her. This was about Clara.

She took a step backwards, her feet cold on

the tiled floor. 'I can't do this,' she whispered. 'I can't stay with you—not when you treat me like this.'

There was no getting away from it. Missy felt used and abused. There was something so primitive about it. He didn't want her. They'd slept together again and he didn't want her. Not like she wanted him. And it hurt. It hurt so much.

She turned to leave but he grabbed her arm. 'You can't leave. You're still having hypos. You need someone to keep an eye on you.' It was the first time that morning his voice held any semblance of warmth.

Missy took a deep breath, raised her eyes to meet his. 'What I need, Cooper, is someone who can look out for my physical and *emotional* health. Someone who can be there for me.' Her hands rested on her stomach. 'And that's not you.'

'Yes, it is.' The words shot out. There was almost desperation in them. He ran his hands through his hair. They were trembling.

She could see he was struggling. She should feel sympathy for him, pity even, but she couldn't. Not now, not like this.

He took a deep breath. 'This is my fault,' he said, his eyes still not quite meeting hers. 'I've confused things. I've made things complicated.'

'By sleeping together?'

He nodded.

'But we'd already done that, Cooper.'

'Not like this.' He spread his arms. 'Last time around, it was for fun. We didn't expect there to be any consequences. We didn't know each other.'

Missy was trying her best to keep her cool. 'And now?'

'This time it's different.' His words finally seemed to make sense to him and he raised his eyes to meet hers. 'I asked you to stay because I wanted to make sure that you and our baby would be healthy. Last night should never have happened. And that's my fault. I'm sorry. We have to go back. We have to sleep in separate rooms.'

Melissa could feel her heart pounding in her chest. She wasn't sorry. She didn't feel sorry at all. She only felt confused. She hadn't come here for a relationship. She hadn't wanted a relationship. But somewhere along the line her feelings had started to change. She wasn't sure what she wanted any more. He was right—last night had confused things. Her head started to spin and she felt herself sway.

'Melissa? Are you all right?' He caught her in his arms and sat her down at the kitchen table. He opened the fridge and pulled out some jam, grabbing the toast that he'd buttered and dumping a huge spoonful on top, before setting it in front of her. 'Eat.'

He dunked a teabag in a cup before adding a spoonful of sugar and placing it next to her, before sitting down opposite her.

Melissa had started mechanically lifting the toast to her mouth. She wasn't even sure if she was having a hypo or if she just felt light-headed because of the events.

'Missy, I'm sorry. I'm supposed to be looking after you.'

She lifted her eyes to meet his. Nothing made sense to her any more. Everything seemed too complicated.

Cooper reached over and took her hand. 'Don't move out. Not when things are like this. Please don't do anything that will put you and the baby at risk.'

He was pleading with her, she could see it in his eyes. This time he was speaking from the heart. She'd started to think he didn't have a heart.

She nodded numbly, her hand falling automatically to her stomach. He was right. She wasn't ready to be her own yet and no matter how much it hurt her, she couldn't do anything to hurt their baby.

CHAPTER EIGHT

'READY?'

Cooper pulled the car into the staff car park and turned off the engine.

Missy nodded nervously and pulled her bag from the floor of the car.

Today was their appointment for their detailed scan of the baby. The scan that would tell them if everything looked okay. If the brain, spine and organs were formed properly, if the bones were in proportion.

The first picture had already been replaced by another at fifteen weeks, and a second at nineteen weeks. In each picture the little image had grown in size and had become a little bit clearer. The red frame sat in pride of place in the middle of the coffee table, the first thing that anyone who entered the flat would see.

And Missy was still there. Still staying at the flat and still sleeping in a separate bedroom.

She and Cooper had fallen into an awkward routine. Her hypoglycaemic attacks were beginning to settle. Missy had managed to get herself back on an even keel and, as much as she didn't want to admit it, living with Cooper seemed to have helped. They did the shopping together and took turns making dinner. If they were working the same shifts they travelled to and from work together. Every night he ran her a warm bath to soothe her aching legs and feet. Companionable. That was how she would describe their relationship. But it made them sound like an elderly couple. The truth was the sexual tension continued to run between them like a gentle undercurrent. Every now and then, hands would brush together with the familiar zing of electricity sparking between them, only to be hastily retracted.

And Melissa would remind herself once more, *This is only temporary.* But something inside her was changing. And she didn't know how it had happened or when it had happened. Maybe it was the pregnancy, or the pregnancy hormones, but something was making her wonder about being on her own. Was it really what she wanted? Or was she beginning to want something more?

She stared at the figure walking ahead of her along the hospital corridor. Once again, Cooper was lost in his own thoughts. And once again Melissa felt as if she was excluded.

Fiona was on duty in the scan room again and she settled Melissa comfortably on the couch, before dimming the lights and readying the scanner.

'All set?'

Melissa gave her a little nod. Her body had gradually swollen over the last few weeks and nothing really fitted her any more. She was resisting the temptation to ask for maternity-style uniforms. They made anyone who wore them look like a giant walking white tent. Instead she'd traded tunic tops with a friend who was a size bigger than her and had recently lost some weight, although that didn't help her with the trousers, which would no longer fasten around her waist. Instead she'd had to content herself with leaving the top button unfastened.

Missy stared down at the little bump with pride, her hand automatically resting on her swollen abdomen. A smile crept across her lips as she felt the little flutterings of movement underneath her fingertips. She gestured to Cooper.

In the darkness Cooper moved his warm hand over hers, laying his fingers in between hers as he tried to feel the light movements under her skin.

'Can you feel it yet?' she whispered. It had become a standing joke between them that Cooper couldn't feel the baby's movements yet. From the moment Missy had first felt the little quickenings around eighteen weeks she had encouraged him to press his hand on her stomach to try and feel the baby moving.

Cooper shook his head with a wry smile. 'No, not yet.' He moved his hand out of the way as Fiona squirted some gel on Missy's stomach and placed the scanner in position.

'Let's get a good look at this baby,' said Fiona decisively.

Missy held her breath. This was her fourth scan and she still held her breath every time the scanner was held in place. She knew she had no reason to worry—her blood-sugar levels had been good, never rising to levels that could put their baby's development at risk. All her other tests had shown she was at low risk of certain genetic conditions, so she knew there was no reason to worry, but it didn't stop her.

The picture appeared clearly on the screen. 'Okay, folks, you know the routine. I'm just going to check all of baby's organs and check the size and weight measurements again.' Fiona turned and faced them both. 'So the million-dollar question is—do you want to know the sex of your baby?'

Missy gulped. She knew this question had been coming. Most midwives were quite traditional and didn't want to know what they were having—they wanted 'a surprise'. But Missy didn't want a surprise. She wanted to plan. She wanted to ask her mother to knit her little cardigans in pale pink or pale blue wool. She wanted to buy her baby a gorgeous outfit to come home from hospital in. Not the plain and boring white or lemon. She wanted colour to reflect the sex of her baby.

But fear flooded her. How would Cooper feel if it was a little girl? Missy bit her bottom lip. 'What do you think, Cooper?' she asked nervously. 'Should we find out?'

Cooper looked at her face and a knot turned in his stomach. He knew she wanted to know. He had dreaded this. He started saying silent prayers in his head. Prayers for a son. Another baby girl would just bring back the pain of losing Lily and he didn't want that. He couldn't tell Missy, though. She was becoming more and more twitchy as the pregnancy progressed. She was trying to pretend she was relaxed about the whole thing, but he could see the internet searches she'd done in his absence or when she'd had one of his well-thumbed obstetric books out, examining some hidden complaint in detail. He'd seen the pile of notes she'd made. She seemed to be obsessed by statistics. Diabetes and pregnancy complications statistics. How much more likely she was to have pre-eclampsia, premature labour, congenital malformations—the list was endless—because of her diabetes.

He reached over in the darkness and squeezed her hand. 'Whatever you want to do is fine with me, Missy.'

Missy glanced between his face and Fiona, who was patiently waiting for an answer.

'Well,' she started hesitantly, 'I think that—'

'We may as well find out,' cut in Cooper, trying to take the pressure off Missy. 'It makes sense as we'll probably be able to see during the scan anyway.' He gave Fiona a little nod of his head to acknowledge the fact she'd probably been dreading doing this scan, as it was likely that at some point the secret would have been revealed. It would be difficult for an experienced midwife like Missy and an obstetrician like Cooper to fail to notice.

Fiona continued to move the scanner across Missy's abdomen. 'There's the heart.' She pointed it out, monitoring the blood flow through the heart and giving them both a little smile. 'The head and brain all look normal. The spine looks good, well formed, everything intact. That little black circle is the baby's bladder.' She gave Missy a smile. 'Obviously full.'

A smile passed between Missy and Cooper, a smile of relief. Everything was good, their baby was healthy. Fiona took a few more notes. 'Growth and weight look normal for twenty-one weeks.' She swept the scanner lower down Missy's abdomen. 'Now, if baby will oblige we'll have a look to see if it's a he or a she. Yup, there we are, folks, say hello to Miss Roberts.'

A girl. The breath caught in her throat. She'd always wanted a little girl but had been afraid to say those words to Cooper. She could have a whole house filled with pink things. She could buy stripy tights. She could have a bobble-bag, a bag filled with hair bobbles to match every outfit. She could get her mum to knit one of those gorgeous baby hats, pale pink with the fluffy pink caribou around the rim. Or even better, one of the pom-pom hats, with a huge pom-pom practically the same size as the baby's head. All the things she'd said she'd never do. She'd almost missed the fact that Fiona had referred to her daughter as 'Miss Roberts'. They hadn't talked about surnames yet. But she was excited. She was having a girl. Wonderful.

But how would Cooper feel? Her eyes strained through the darkness of the scan room to try and catch the expression on his face.

A girl. Cooper felt a dagger of ice pierce his heart. The blade dug deeper and deeper, to be replaced by a tight cold hand, squeezing his heart so fiercely that the breath was struggling to leave his lungs. Lily. The small blue-tinged baby who should have been rosy and pink. The pale, perfect skin, dark hair and gorgeous features that had never been destined to draw breath in this world. And now two years later he was having another girl—once again, it felt like a betrayal.

'Cooper? Are you all right?' she whispered.

Conscious of his behaviour and her reaction previously, he squeezed Missy's hand and shot her a smile. 'Of course I am. We'll need to start thinking of names,' he said, trying to be enthusiastic.

'Yes,' she agreed, nodding her head while deep in thought.

'Missy?' Fiona started to wipe the gel from

Missy's stomach. 'Would you like to come in next door and we'll get you a gorgeous picture of your daughter's face on the 3D scanner?'

'Oh, yes, please.' Missy edged herself off the examination couch and pulled her trousers up again. 'Coming, Coop?'

'Sure.'

They headed into the next door room and waited patiently while Fiona adjusted the scanner until they'd managed to capture a picture of their daughter's face. She printed the scans off for them and handed them to Cooper, who quickly placed one inside the plastic folder that held Missy's midwifery notes, pushing the second one into his coat pocket.

'We'll put that in our frame,' he said giving her a quiet smile. 'I need to head along and do my clinic. I'll come along and see you later.'

She leaned forward and brushed against his hand, 'Cooper, are you okay?'

He gave her a tight smile, one that didn't reach his eyes and made him look as if a mask had been painted on his face.

Her heart squeezed. For once she didn't want

to be at arm's length from him. He was hurting. She wanted to let him know she understood.

She wrapped her arms around his neck and whispered in his ear, 'I know this would have been easier on you if it was a boy. But this is different. This is our daughter, not Lily. And everything will be fine this time.'

She saw him shift uncomfortably as she spoke, but she had to say something. She couldn't for a second read what was going on inside his mind.

'It's fine, Missy. Honestly, it is. Now, I need to get to my clinic.'

Missy grasped the plastic folder in her hands and watched his figure retreating down the corridor. The scan room may have been dark but she'd seen the fleeting expression on his face. She also knew that he'd tried to hide his reaction from her. And she was trying to understand, truly she was. But she just wanted him to be as happy as she was and sing from the rooftops that they were having a baby girl. Was that so wrong?

But the truth of the matter was she didn't understand. And no matter how uncomfortable their relationship was, Cooper had a right to be involved. Maybe she was just being hormonal? She could feel an ache in the pit of her stomach. He'd said all the right things but he hadn't been able to hide what had been in his eyes. Missy felt as if she was dangling on a cliff edge and the slightest push could send her tumbling into oblivion. She'd never felt so alone.

Cooper walked along the hallway, his mind in turmoil and his stomach churning. A hand reached out and grabbed him.

'Cooper?' Dave Hammond, an anaesthetist, was standing in front of him, his glance down the corridor on where Missy stood, staring out of one of the nearby windows. She looked lost and Dave's brow furrowed. 'Did everything go all right at the scan?'

Cooper nodded distractedly. 'Yes, yes, everything went fine.' He followed Dave's gaze down the corridor. 'Were you looking for me?'

Dave nodded. 'We need you in Theatre for an emergency section in around ten minutes.' He looked back towards Melissa. 'You do know you're an idiot, don't you Coop?'

Cooper's eyebrows shot upwards, taken aback by the normally placid Dave's words. 'What do you mean?'

Dave gestured down the corridor towards Melissa. 'Word travels fast, Coop. I know you lost your first wife and I'm sorry—truly I am. But you've got a second chance at happiness right in front of you and you're a fool not to take it.'

Cooper shook his head. 'You can't understand. It's complicated…'

'So's life.'

Cooper started at the blunt words.

Dave continued. 'My old dad was devastated when my mum died giving birth to me. He spent thirty years as a widower—he was never lucky enough to meet someone else—but he always told me if he'd ever met someone who gave him the same spark he'd had with Mum, he would grab her with both hands. You have the opportunity right in front of you, Cooper, but you're too big a fool to take it.' Dave shook his head. 'You're so lost in being miserable that you can't move on.' He gestured back to the forlorn figure of Melissa, who had picked up her bag and was slowly walking towards the exit door at the bottom of the corridor. 'Life's too short. It's for living, Coop—so go and live it.'

Dave turned and walked back towards the theatre doors, leaving a stunned Cooper in his wake.

Cooper's eyes followed Melissa as she pushed open the door. His eyes lingered on her rapidly expanding stomach. What had started as a gentle swell was now a well-defined bump. Twenty-one weeks. *His baby.* And the thought didn't fill him with panic, or dread.

He watched as she exited out into the brilliant sunshine, the opened door filling the corridor with a sharp stream of sunlight that disappeared as the door slammed closed behind her. It was almost symbolic. He wanted to run along the corridor and grab her. What was wrong with him? Why couldn't he just give himself a shake and move on?

He looked down at the piece of paper he'd pulled from his pocket. An updated scan image of his daughter. His finger traced the little outline in front of him. This was where he needed to concentrate his thoughts. This was his priority.

Melissa was a strong, independent woman. She wouldn't wait for him forever. She might not wait for him at all.

It was time to get his house in order.

Last night's jeans lay in a crumpled heap on the floor and Cooper picked them up to toss them in the laundry basket. Something fell from his pocket, something glistening and gold. Cooper bent down and picked up his wedding ring.

He turned the ring over and over between his fingers. Taking it off had been a huge step but now it was time for something else. Now Melissa and their expected baby had moved in. It might only be on a temporary basis but if the truth be told, it was the push that he needed. It was time. He knew it was time. His heart twisted as he realised that it hadn't been Clara who'd been haunting his dreams for a while now. No, now his dreams were filled with a woman with beautiful emerald green eyes and chestnut hair. For a second he felt guilty. Was he forgetting Clara? Was he forgetting their time together? No, those memories would always be with him. But maybe, subconsciously, he was finally letting her go.

He had to make an effort. He had to stop holding Missy and the baby at arm's length. His eyes fell on a bunch of brochures sitting on the arm of the sofa. He knew exactly how to do it.

He held up the ring. For a second it caught a ray of sunlight streaming through the window, sending a warm reflection of gold onto the nearby wall. Cooper brought the ring to his lips and gave it a little kiss, then stood up, opened one of his nearby drawers and dropped it inside. Little by little, he was getting there.

They pulled up in front of the huge warehouse and Cooper turned to where Missy sat in the passenger seat, her hand held over her face. 'Okay, you can open your eyes now.'

She moved her hand and her eyes flickered open. She'd been squeezing them so tightly it took a second for the large, colourful sign to come into focus. A smile spread across her face. 'You brought me here?'

Cooper returned her smile. 'It seemed like the right time. Ready to go and take a look?'

Melissa nodded as he came around and helped her from the car. This was the last place she'd thought he would bring her. She'd wanted to visit the nursery warehouse for a while now, but hadn't wanted to tempt fate. Now she'd had her detailed scan and knew that everything was fine, it seemed like the ideal time.

They pushed open the doors and went inside. Her eyes swept over the wide expanse. For as far as the eye could see there were prams, cots, high chairs and every kind of baby paraphernalia that had ever been invented.

'Wow, where do we start?' asked Melissa as she looked around in wonder.

Cooper shrugged his shoulders. 'I guess wherever you want.'

She wandered among the nursery furniture, picking up brochures and stopping to look at various bedding sets and mobiles. Cooper followed her, dutifully nodding and smiling at everything she suggested.

'I suppose you want everything to be pink?' he

asked as she picked up yet another pink border, before setting it down and moving on to the next.

'Well, not everything,' she said as she pointed in the direction of the prams. 'I've kind of got my heart set on a red pram.'

'Red?'

'I didn't think you'd want to push a pink pram.' She raised her eyebrow at him. 'You are going to be pushing a pram, aren't you, Cooper?'

'Of course. Of course I am.' He moved towards the sea of prams ahead of them. 'But you could be right, preferably not a pink one.'

Melissa walked over to one of red prams and ran her fingers over the hood. 'Yes, definitely red.' Her eyebrows lifted mischievously. 'And you do realise that the rules will apply.'

Cooper felt himself being sucked in. 'And what rules might that be?'

'New pram, new coat.'

He gave a little smile. 'If you wanted a new red coat, all you had to do was say so.' He walked around the brightly coloured pram. It was definitely a safer option than the pink version.

His eyes glanced over at the larger, more traditional prams. 'I thought you might have wanted something a little bigger. My mum had one of those.' He nodded in the direction of the carriage-built prams.

Melissa smiled. 'My mum had one of those too,' she said. 'But I hardly think it's practical for us—we both live in flats.' She looked over the large pram. 'I wouldn't be able to get that up my stairs.'

'You won't need to.' Cooper's voice was steady and determined.

Her eyes widened and she tucked a chestnut curl behind her ear. 'What do you mean?' Her voice was trembling, ever so slightly.

Cooper put his arm around her shoulder, tucking her under his. 'Why would you want to go back to your flat? Don't you like staying with me?'

She held her breath. What had brought this on? 'My diabetes is much more stable now. I haven't had a hypo in weeks.' She reached up and gently touched the side of his cheek. 'I think it's safe for me to go home now.'

'You are home,' he said instantly. His hand encircled the finger that was touching his cheek. 'I want you to stay, you and our baby.' He pointed across the array of baby goods. 'Pick what you like. I was thinking that we should use the other bedroom that overlooks the marina for our daughter. What do you think?'

Melissa felt herself torn in two. On one side she was elated. They'd never spoken about this. Moving in had been a temporary arrangement. On the other side she loved her independence, and she still wasn't sure what she meant to him. She wasn't ready to give up her flat, her security, for a man who was still unsure of his feelings. She'd already been burned once this year and wasn't sure she could deal with it again. More than that. She was terrified. 'I need to give it some thought,' she said quietly. 'This isn't really the kind of place we should be having a discussion like this.' She waved her arm around the nursery warehouse.

Cooper looked at her carefully. He raised his eyebrows. 'What's the point in having two of everything if we don't need it?'

Was that all this meant? A practical solution?

Missy shook her head. 'Cooper, I'm not ready to think that far ahead.' She picked up a nearby brochure. 'I'm not sure what you want from me. While I'm happy to help you decorate the nursery at the flat, I'm still going to buy some things for the baby to keep at my flat.' She leaned backwards, resting her arms against a wooden cot. 'We're not exactly a couple, are we?' She folded her arms across her chest. 'You need to give me some time to think about this…' she ran her hands over her stomach '…but, in the meantime, we'll stay a few more weeks.'

'Good,' said Cooper, letting out the breath he'd been holding. He had no idea what she'd been about to say. He was trying to make an effort. He was trying in every way that he could to move this relationship along, in its most natural sense. He felt protective towards Missy. He wanted to make sure that she and the baby were fine. He glanced around him, looking for any kind of distraction to keep him from the thoughts currently running through his brain. His eyes caught sight of another bright red pram nearby. 'So what about this one?'

She gave a little smile at his quick change of subject. 'I fancy something a little more practical. One where the car seat can be attached onto the frame and has a separate carrycot part.'

He ran his eyes over the light-framed pram. 'Do you think it will be sturdy enough?'

'What do you mean?'

He folded his arms across his chest. 'Well, my mum used her pram for five of us. It lasted for years.' His eyes narrowed at the pram in front of him. 'I'm not sure this thing will be that robust.' He gave the pram a little shake, as if to emphasise his point.

She gave a little laugh. 'I'm not sure about you, Coop, but I'm only planning on using this pram for one baby.' She gave him a mischievous glance. 'Are you planning on selling it on? In an online auction maybe?'

He groaned. His late-night buying habits had been rumbled. 'How many parcels arrived today?'

She wagged her finger at him. 'Three, but then, while I was out, a card was put through the door for another.' She rummaged through her bag and pulled out the dog-eared card. 'Here, you can go for that one yourself.' She gave a little start. 'Quick!' She grabbed hold of his hand and placed it on her stomach. 'There! Do you feel it now?'

Even with his hand over her thin silver top Cooper could feel the delicate ripples of movement beneath the skin on her stomach. He couldn't wipe the smile from his face. Although he'd seen her on the scans it was the first time he'd felt their daughter move. He'd watched her little outline fill out and become more defined as the weeks progressed. But this was even more real. This was happening right now.

Melissa's eyes were shining brightly. 'Can you feel her?'

He nodded enthusiastically. 'I sure can.'

Melissa continued, the excitement evident on her face. 'I just feel so different now. Before I had the last scan, I was so worried.' She placed her hand over his. 'You know—that something might be wrong. But now we've had it and I know everything looks good, I feel as if I can finally plan for the future.' She waved her arm around the shop. 'I've been too terrified to come in anywhere like this. I didn't want to start ordering anything until I knew everything was all right. It's such a relief.'

Cooper took her in his arms and pulled her close.

Melissa took a deep breath and wrapped her arms around his waist. His hand was on her abdomen again, feeling their daughter dancing within. His deep brown eyes were shining with no hint of the shadow that sometimes crossed them. His mouth creased into a smile that showed his perfect white teeth. A genuine smile. Their baby was healthy, but what about their relationship? Right now they had an unbreakable bond. One that would keep them together forever. So why did it feel so fragile?

CHAPTER NINE

MELISSA was in a state of bliss. She was in the middle of the impossibly comfortable red sofa surrounded by baby catalogues. She'd spent the whole morning looking at cots, wardrobes, baby chairs, changing stations, curtains and bedding. She stared out the window across the marina. This place was really starting to feel like home. She was getting used to waking up to the spectacular view. But somewhere, deep inside her, there was still the distinct feeling of unease. She looked at the lists she'd made for baby items—one for her flat and one for Cooper's. She needed that. Needed that security. She needed to know that everything was in place for her and her baby, no matter where she was and what happened.

She stood up and walked through to the third bedroom, which had last night been designated the baby's room. Like the rest of the flat, it had plain white walls. She brushed her fingers along the wall as she walked over to the window. This bedroom was bigger than the living room in her one-bedroom flat. She'd barely visited her flat since moving in with Cooper, only checking in once a week to pick up her mail and ensure everything was secure. The tiniest knot formed in the bottom of her stomach. She imagined herself crammed into her tiny flat, surrounded by baby things. It would be a tight squeeze—the cot would have to be squashed into her bedroom. Now it seemed as if that might never happen. Could she really stay here with their daughter? Cooper had asked her again and she still hadn't given him an answer. The truth was that she really didn't need to stay any more. Her diabetes was under control. She hadn't had a hypoglycaemic attack in four weeks. It was safe for her to be on her own again. But did she want to be?

Melissa ran her hands over her bulging stomach. *Their daughter.* Even the thought brought a smile to her lips. She was twenty-six weeks now and she finally felt secure enough to start buying things for her arrival. The bottom drawer of her bedside cabinet was stuffed with pink socks, tiny white vests with little pink bows, a pink knitted cardigan her mother had given her, plus the gorgeous pink pom-pom hat she'd imagined. Every few days some other little treasure would be added to the pile, and Melissa would once again take everything out the drawer, one by one, smiling at the idea that one day soon her daughter would be wearing these clothes.

But for some strange reason Melissa hadn't felt able to share the excitement of her clothes buying with Cooper—and she wasn't quite sure why.

He was still being wonderful to her. Running her baths and helping make dinner most evenings. If he had to work late, he would phone her to make sure she was fine, often offering to pick up dinner on the way home. And his fan club seemed to be growing on a daily basis. He was an excellent doctor. He was conscientious and listened to both his colleagues and his patients. He seemed to have good instincts and had picked up on a number of unusual cases that could have had tricky outcomes if he had not intervened. Above all, people seemed to like him. To all intents and purposes, Cooper was the perfect partner.

But everything wasn't quite perfect. They still slept in separate rooms. In separate beds. At times it felt as if Cooper was scared to touch her. Sure, he would rub her back if it was sore, give her the occasional hug, even touch her stomach when the baby was kicking. But he didn't kiss her. He didn't touch her. Not in the way she wanted to be touched.

Melissa looked around the room again. She ran her hand along the pristine white wall once more. It would look nice in a shade of pale pink. Her eyes flickered to one of the brochures she'd left lying on the bed. Would she need one wardrobe or two? There was a built-in cupboard at one end of the room and she pulled the door open to get a feel for the space inside.

It was huge, with a rail for hanging clothes and a variety of shelves at the back. Her hand flicked on the switch just inside the door and the dark space was immediately filled with light. She stepped right inside. Wow! There was loads of storage space in here, none of it currently being used.

Then her eyes were caught by a cardboard box in the bottom right-hand corner of the cupboard. She knelt down beside it and pulled the box towards her. What was this doing in here? Maybe it was some kitchen equipment that Cooper had forgotten about? From the scarcity of items in the kitchen it seemed most likely. He had mentioned that he'd lost a box somewhere in the move.

She unfolded the four cardboard leaves of the box and stared at the contents. No, it definitely wasn't kitchen utensils. It was a strange array of items. She pulled out the first. A little porcelain ornament of a children's carousel. It was gorgeous. A red canopy with rows of different-coloured horses underneath, all mounted on red and white poles. She ran her fingers over the delicate ornament. Maybe it was a childhood memento? Or a family heirloom? It was difficult to judge the age of an item like this. She placed it carefully to one side and reached in for the next item. A small black velvet box.

Melissa's breath caught in her throat and her

fingers trembled. All of a sudden she knew she shouldn't be doing this. She automatically glanced over her shoulder, as if she might be caught in the act. But there was no one there. Cooper was working at the hospital. She was alone.

Her eyes went back back to the box. No matter how much her head told her she shouldn't be looking at this, she opened the box. An engagement ring. A beautiful pink diamond glistened in the velvet lining. It must have been Clara's. Her fingers touched the thin gold band and stunning diamond.

Melissa snapped the box shut. This was private. Cooper had obviously put these things in here to try to forget. She should put them away and push the box back into the corner.

But she couldn't. She couldn't bear not to look in the box.

Her hands found the next item. It was heavy and she needed two hands to lift it out. It was a wedding album. Melissa gently unwrapped the delicate tissue paper surrounding the album. A photograph was inlaid into the black leather cover. A heart-shaped photograph of a happy couple, their arms wrapped around each other on a beautiful summer's day.

Melissa felt as if an arrow had pierced her heart. Cooper looked so young. She peered closely at the photograph before carefully opening the cover. On the first page was Clara, with an older man, probably her father, standing beside a silver Bentley. She had long blonde hair and beautiful blue eyes. Her dress was straight, with pearls encrusted around the pale bodice and a satin skirt. She had a sparkling tiara and short veil and carried a spray of pale pink roses in her hand. But more than all that, she glowed. The smile from her pretty lips reached all the way up into her eyes.

Melissa felt a sharp kick in her abdomen. Clara looked totally different from her. Small, blonde and blue eyed. Melissa's hand subconsciously reached up to touch her chestnut curls. They were totally different. Her brain started to scream in her ears. If he liked small blondes, what was he doing with her? Her hand went to her stomach.

Again, the thought flew into her head: *Was he only with her because of the baby?*

She knew she should stop, but she couldn't. Melissa kept turning the pages, each one more heartbreaking than the one before. Cooper standing outside the church, waiting for his bride. Cooper and Jake, his best man, shaking hands outside the church. The bride and groom standing on the church steps, holding out their hands to show their wedding rings, the pink diamond clearly visible on Clara's finger. Cooper and Clara standing in the middle of a park, their arms around each other, throwing back their heads and laughing.

Melissa felt the hot tears spill down her cheeks. One splodged on the photograph she was looking at and she hurriedly wiped it away. Cooper looked so young and carefree. The little lines that were currently around his eyes and forehead were nowhere in sight in these pictures. The dark expression that could flit across his face at the most inopportune moments, before disappearing again in the blink of an eye, looked as if it had never been present when these pictures had been taken. Then there were the shadowed moments when he thought that no one was watching him and he looked as if he had the weight of the world on his shoulders.

None of those expressions were present in these photographs. Melissa continued to flick through the album. Cooper and Clara cutting their wedding cake, Cooper and Clara having their first dance, and finally the one that sliced her heart in two. Cooper and Clara caught in a private moment, staring deeply into one another's eyes. A couple clearly in love, with their whole future ahead of them.

And then there were others at the back of the album. Pictures from their honeymoon. A picture of Clara standing with her hand outstretched, pretending to hold up the Leaning Tower of Pisa. Melissa dropped the picture in shock. She was having flashbacks. A few weeks earlier she'd told Cooper she would love to visit Pisa and she'd seen something flit across his face. The pieces of the jigsaw puzzle were slowly fitting into place. The tears were flowing freely now. Melissa felt sick, not only from seeing how happy Cooper had been but also for the intrusion. She'd invaded his privacy. He'd put these pictures in this cupboard for a reason. They were too painful to look at. For him, and for her.

She pushed the album back into the box. There were other items still wrapped in tissue paper but she'd seen enough. She couldn't bear to look at anything else. Melissa shoved the box back into the corner of the cupboard and closed the door, resting back against it, as if to try and seal it from her thoughts. She pulled a handkerchief from her pocket to wipe her tears. All of a sudden she couldn't imagine the cool white room transformed into a warm pink nursery. Nothing about this seemed right.

Melissa slammed shut the catalogues on the bed. She couldn't bear to think about nursery furniture, or anything else for that matter.

As the hot angry tears continued to slip down her cheeks Melissa came to a startling conclusion. What had started out as a relationship of convenience had become something much more. The giant fist that was currently gripping and squeezing at her heart hadn't arrived overnight.

Although their initial attraction had been instant and fleeting, their relationship had changed over the past few months. It had grown. So had her feelings.

She was in love. She was in love with Cooper, the father of her baby and the man who clearly still had to get over his wife. This was a love that had her on top of the world at one moment and at the bottom of a dark pit in the next. She'd never felt anything like this for David. She'd never felt a love that made her stomach ache like this. Melissa felt a little kick inside, as if her daughter was protesting at her mother's tears. She walked over to the window. As she stared out over at the bustling marina Melissa knew one thing. Baby or no baby, Clara's shadow was hanging over her like a black, looming cloud and until she was gone it felt as if she and Cooper could never move on to the next stage of their relationship.

The tears fell freely down her cheeks. She couldn't go on living her life in limbo. She didn't want to be his second choice. She didn't want to have Cooper because she was pregnant with his child. She wanted to have him because he was *hers*.

She walked through to the white bedroom and pulled a bag from the cupboard—the same bag that she'd used weeks ago when she'd moved in. She started pulling clothes from the hangers in the cupboard and stuffing them into the bag. Shirts, dresses, trousers and all the new things that Cooper had purchased for her, all crushed into the bag. She didn't want to waste time. She should have done this weeks ago when he'd shut her out after they'd slept together. She didn't want to pack neatly and in an orderly fashion. She wanted to get out of here while she still had the courage to do it.

She pulled another bag from the cupboard and started throwing underwear and nightclothes from the bedside cabinet into it.

In ten minutes she was finished. The only trace left of her was the unmade bed and the red-framed ultrasound picture in the living room. She picked up her bags and walked through to the kitchen. She would write him a note.

Her mind shifted. She wasn't going to make

any excuses. She was going to tell him exactly why she was leaving. She walked back through to the other bedroom, the bedroom that should be for their child, and picked up the box. She placed it on the kitchen counter, pulled out a pad and pen from one of the drawers and started to write.

Cooper bounded up the stairs, two at a time. He was home early and planned to take Missy out for dinner. He opened the heavy wooden door and stopped short.

Missy was at the kitchen counter, her face streaked with tears and two bags at her feet.

'What's going on?' He was breathless from running up the stairs. 'What are you doing, Missy?'

Her eyes met his. Something was different. It was almost as if her vitality and spark had been drained out of her. 'I'm leaving.'

'You're *what*?' He crossed the kitchen in two steps. 'What on earth are you talking about?'

Missy put down the pen with a trembling hand and pushed the box in his direction. 'I can't live here, Cooper. You don't love me. You fell into this relationship, but you can't commit to it. I don't need you to explain, I know that you're still in love with your wife. But that's not enough for me. I want everything, and that includes your love.'

Cooper was dumbfounded. Then he saw it on the kitchen worktop. The box. She'd found the box. The one he'd hidden away in the back of cupboard somewhere. He hadn't thought about the box for months. He'd almost forgotten it was there. 'But, Missy—'

She raised her hand. 'Don't, Cooper. Don't make this harder than it already is. I need to get away from you.' She drew her hands across her stomach. 'I need to prepare myself for our baby coming. I need to sort all this out in my head.'

Cooper's words stuck in his mouth. This was it. This was the time that he was supposed to tell her that he loved her. That would stop her leaving. That would make her stay.

But the words choked him. He couldn't get them out. She'd taken him by surprise. He hadn't expected this and he wasn't prepared for it. All the thoughts and emotions that Missy evoked in him came bubbling to the surface. But what did they mean? He hesitated for too long, because she bent and picked up her bags.

'I want you to stay, Missy,' he said, as his voice broke and he reached for her arm.

She felt as if she were eleven years old again. She felt the pain sear through her heart as it had when her father had walked out the door. The one thing she had vowed to protect herself from, the one thing she had never wanted to feel again.

'But we don't always get what we want, Cooper,' she said as she held her head high and walked out of the door.

CHAPTER TEN

THE phone rang at the midwives' station and Melissa picked it up quickly. 'Hello, Labour Ward, Sister Bell.' Andrea had just walked down the corridor and started to say something to her but Melissa held up her hand to silence her. She lifted a pen and paper and took some notes. 'Yes, how long? From where? We'll be on standby.'

She replaced the receiver. 'We're getting a transfer from the General Hospital A and E. Lydia Jones, twenty-four, thirty-seven weeks pregnant, with a suspected PE. She's apparently in a bad way; one of the surgical registrars is in the ambulance with her. We're going to need a team down here stat.'

Andrea gave a quick nod, moving instantly into professional mode. 'You page the anaesthetist and Cooper, I'll organise the room and the midwifery staff.'

She sped off down the corridor. Melissa picked up the phone, her hand trembling as she paged Cooper and Dave Hammond. Pulmonary embolism, or a clot in the lungs, was one of the leading causes of maternal death. It was very serious for both the mother and the baby. How would Cooper react—treating a woman with the same condition that had killed his wife and baby? Time would be of the essence here and it was essential the correct team of people was assembled to give Lydia and her baby the best possible chance of survival.

She sighed. Lydia was thirty-seven weeks, she herself had another ten weeks before she'd reach that stage. Her hand went automatically to her stomach. It was getting harder and harder to work in the labour ward. Physically, she was feeling fine, but mentally she was starting to struggle with some of the more intense deliveries she was dealing with. This last week had been the hardest yet, especially when every time she saw Cooper she thought her heart might break. At the last count there had been forty phone calls, over a hundred texts and three visits to her flat. But he still hadn't said the words. The three little words she need to hear.

And being at work wasn't helping. Her mind was working overtime. If the labours and deliveries she was attending went well, she would be overjoyed, or maybe it was relieved. If complications arose, with more serious outcomes for the mother or the baby, Melissa would instantly imagine herself being in that position. What if that was her? What if something happened to her baby?

She knew she shouldn't worry. Things were going well. Her last scan had showed the baby to be a little larger than normal, but that could be expected in diabetic pregnancies and the baby's growth was still within normal limits. And let's face it, she had a consultant obstetrician who constantly fussed around her. She was in good hands. Even if they weren't his hands...

The phone jolted her out of her wandering thoughts. 'Labour Ward... Hi, Cooper, we're going to need you down here. We're getting a transfer from the General's A and E department, a thirty-seven-weeker with a suspected PE. Cooper? Cooper? Did you hear me?'

All Melissa could hear at the end of the phone was a deafening silence. Cooper was always on the ball and rarely ever distracted. But this was a PE. This was what had killed his wife and child. She glanced at her watch. He would be in the antenatal clinic right now, maybe one of the midwives was speaking to him. She gave it another few seconds. 'Cooper?' She lowered her voice. 'Are you okay? ETA is ten minutes. It must be serious as one of the surgical registrars is with her in the ambulance. Can you make your way down here, please?' She tried to make it sound like business as usual, even though she knew it wasn't.

Cooper mumbled something in reply. The other phone at the midwives' station started to ring. 'That'll be Dave. I'd better get it. See you in a few minutes.'

Cooper stared at the phone in his hand. Melissa had rung off and he could hear the hum of the dead tone. He knew he should replace the phone but he couldn't. He was numb.

As soon as she'd said 'PE' his heart had sunk like a stone. He'd always known that one day this would happen.

He replaced the receiver and sat for a few moments with his head in his hands. He was a professional. He could deal with this. Apart from Melissa, hardly anyone knew about his past. Some knew his wife had died but no one knew his wife had died in his arms of a PE. No one knew that for months he had relived the nightmare over and over in his dreams, waking drenched in sweat and calling out her name. Reaching out for his daughter that they'd been just too late to save.

But those dreams had changed a few months ago. Every night while Melissa lay sleeping, curled up in his arms, his mind would whirr with questions of what if? What if the same thing happened to Melissa? What if he lost a second daughter? Should he have done something different? Why hadn't Clara had any of the normal signs of a PE?

Cooper shook his head. The feelings of self-doubt were surfacing in his mind. He knew he hadn't done anything wrong. He knew he hadn't missed anything with Clara. The post-mortem had confirmed it. It was just 'one of those things'.

The tears were hiding beneath his heavy lids. He was a good doctor. He was an excellent obstetrician. Everyone who worked with him told him that. He knew that in the last few months he'd saved the lives of a number of mothers and their babies. Only an hour ago he'd been called to assist in Theatre when one of the other consultants had run into some problems. All because of his knowledge and skills.

Cooper took a deep breath. He had to pull himself together. Right now, he was the best chance that this woman and her child would have. He had to be at the top of his game. It was time to work. It was time to focus.

He pulled down his white coat, which was hanging behind the door, and threw it over his theatre scrubs, an unreadable expression on his face as he headed down the corridor towards the labour suite.

* * *

The trolley came thundering down the corridor towards Melissa as she unlocked the double doors to the room. Pushed by two red-faced porters and one panting doctor, there was no time to delay. Andrea appeared at her side and together they helped pull the trolley next to the waiting bed.

Cooper walked straight past her and addressed the surgical registrar. 'Give me a report, please.'

The panting doctor took a deep breath. 'This is Lydia Jones, she's twenty-four. Presented with chest pain…' he glanced at his watch '…at the General around twenty minutes ago.' He gestured towards the patient. 'As you can see, she's thirty-seven weeks pregnant.' His eyes flicked to the notes in his hand. 'This is her second child. No underlying medical conditions that we know of, but her condition has deteriorated rapidly in the ambulance in the way over.' He gestured at Lydia's right arm. 'We've got IV access and a full set of bloods have already been sent to the lab as an emergency.' He closed the notes and left them at the foot of the bed. 'The only thing of note she told us was that she suffered from symphysis pubis dysfunction and has been on bed rest the last few weeks.' He pointed to the medical notes he'd left on the bed. 'She arrived without her hand-held midwifery record, so we were unsure of any other problems.'

Andrea gave a quick nod of the head at Cooper and then at Dave, who had just appeared through the door. 'I'll go and find her midwifery records to see if we can get a better picture.'

Melissa walked around to the other side of the bed and, with the rest of the team, helped move Lydia over from the trolley to the bed. She gave Lydia a little smile. 'I'm Melissa, one of the midwives who will be looking after you.' She gestured with her head to her right. 'This is Dave Hammond, the anaesthetist, and over there…' she pointed to the bottom of the bed '…is Cooper Roberts, one of the consultant obstetricians.' She gave Lydia's hand a squeeze. 'Don't worry Lydia, you're in good hands.'

Lydia was a small woman who appeared to be overweight. Her eyes were tightly screwed shut, as if she was trying to block out her surroundings. Her breathing was rapid and shallow. Melissa noted the peripheral oedema in her legs and silently gestured towards Dave, drawing his attention to her condition.

Melissa was struggling to place electrodes on Lydia's chest to monitor her heart rate. Dave instantly went to the side of the bed to give her a hand and to change over from the portable oxygen supply. Melissa's eyes went to Cooper. His face was a complete blank. It seemed impenetrable. Usually he would be the first person to give her a hand. She touched the side of his elbow. She understood that treating a patient with a PE would be difficult for Cooper, but he had a job to do.

'Cooper?'

Cooper was weighing up the options in his head. Most maternity units were attached to general hospitals, but not St Jude's. It had been a specialised maternity hospital for several decades and although the hospital had been updated, not all facilities were available. There was no ITU and no other specialities to assist with patients like this. The General was only five minutes away, but in some situations that five minutes could be the difference between life and death.

He glanced at the surgical registrar. 'Who made the decision to transfer her here?'

The surgical registrar hesitated. 'Well, we weren't sure, but as we don't have facilities for neonates at the General, Mr Graves thought she would be better here.'

Cooper nodded. Mr Graves was a consultant surgeon and would probably have had a heart attack at the thought of Lydia delivering at the General. He was quite sure Mr Graves had arranged for an ambulance to transfer her in a flash. His mind seemed to shift into focus. His head lifted and turned towards Dave. 'Let's make an assessment of our patient.'

They moved quickly. Lydia was pale. Cooper turned to Melissa. 'We need an ECG right now.'

Melissa pulled the electrocardiograph machine from the corner of the room and started placing the leads on Lydia's chest. 'We're just going to do a little tracing of your heart Lydia, it will only take a minute.'

Dave was standing at the side of the bed, a stethoscope clutched in his hand as he listened to Lydia's chest sounds. 'I'm hearing crackles in the chest,' he said as he moved to the head of the bed. 'Her breathing is very shallow and laboured. I would definitely go with a PE.'

Cooper stood at the end of the bed, watching the printout of the ECG. 'Do we have a chest X-ray?'

The surgical registrar nodded and pulled the X-ray from its brown envelope. Cooper stuck it on one of the nearby light boxes and flicked the switch. Dave appeared at his elbow to peer at the film. Cooper raised his finger and pointed at a number of areas on the X-ray. 'It's certainly not a normal chest X-ray but we can't use this as a definitive diagnosis.' He leaned over and tore off the printout of the ECG. 'Abnormal ECG,' he muttered, before handing it over to Dave. 'Sinus tachycardia with ST wave abnormalities. There are also some changes showing right ventricular strain.' He turned his head towards the registrar. 'Did you manage to perform any other tests?'

The registrar shook his head. He gestured to-wards the bed. 'Her condition had deteriorated too much to perform a VQ scan. Our consultant tried to arrange an urgent echocardiogram but the on-call technician hadn't answered their page by the time I left.'

Cooper shook his head in disgust. He knew the latest guidelines for managing PE in pregnancy off by heart. It was essential that an echocardiogram be carried out within the first hour. He pointed towards the door. 'Go and telephone your A and E department to see if the technician has answered their page yet. If they have, tell them to get here *now*. We need this test carried out.'

The registrar nodded quickly and shot out the door.

Dave had resumed his position and continued to listen to Lydia's chest. He'd removed the head of the bed to stand behind Lydia. His face clouded over. 'Coop, I'm hearing a third heart sound and there is a parasternal heave present.'

Melissa's head shot up from where she had just fastened the blood-pressure cuff around Lydia's right arm. Both of those symptoms were clinical signs of a pulmonary embolism. She pressed the button to measure Lydia's blood pressure. The cuff inflated in a matter of seconds. 'She's hypotensive,' she called to Cooper, who appeared lost in thought.

She knew what he was doing—blocking out all memories from the past. It was almost as if he was on autopilot. He walked over to Dave. 'I think we're going to have to thrombolyse her.'

Dave nodded. 'I know. Her respiratory effort is decreasing. I think I'm going to have to intubate her.' He glanced back at the patient. 'This is serious.'

Cooper turned his eyes to the cardiac monitor. 'She's tachycardic and there's a strong possibility we're going to have to take her to Theatre to deliver this baby.'

Andrea walked into the room and handed the midwifery notes over to Cooper. 'Absolutely nothing in them. She's only been on bed rest for the last three weeks. No medical history to predispose her to having a PE. She's been unlucky. It looks like it's just one of those things.'

Cooper felt his blood run cold. *One of those things.* Just like Clara. Before his very eyes the face on the bed morphed into Clara's. It wasn't

Lydia Jones any more, it was Clara. Cooper tried to focus. He had to keep it together.

'Any relatives?'

Andrea checked the notes. 'There was no one with her in the General's A and E. She presented herself with the chest pain. She's given a contact number for her husband. I'll go and try and phone him.'

Cooper walked up to Dave Hammond, speaking in a low voice. 'I don't think the normal IV unfractionated heparin will be enough. It's not going to break up the clot quickly enough to stop there being long-term damage.'

Dave nodded his head. 'I'm in complete agreement with you, Coop, but it's your decision. If she doesn't respond and we have to take her to Theatre, there is real danger that she'll haemorrhage.'

'I know that, but I think the benefits outweigh the risks. Studies have shown that thrombolysis is more effective than heparin therapy in reducing the clot burden and rapidly improving the haemodynamics. The clot could dissolve and she could go on to have a normal delivery in three weeks.'

Cooper turned his head towards Melissa. 'Are you familiar with streptokinase?'

'I'm familiar with it, but I've never used it. I know they stock it in our pharmacy. Do you want me to get some?'

Cooper nodded, his head turning as the surgical registrar came back through the door. 'The technician will be here in five minutes,' said the registrar, who was pulling the echocardiogram machine behind him. 'I decided to go and get this for her to save time.'

Cooper walked back over to his patient. He touched her arm gently, trying to entice her to open her eyes. 'Lydia, I know that you're scared, but I need to explain what's going to happen. We think you might have a blood clot in your lungs.'

Her eyes flew open, terror registering on her face.

Cooper spoke slowly, trying to allay her fears. 'We've treated women with blood clots before. Things are a little trickier in your case as you're so near to your delivery date.'

Lydia opened her mouth, her breathing in short gasps. 'Why would I get a blood clot?'

'There could be a number of reasons. We know that you suffer from symphysis pubis dysfunction and that you've been unable to get about for the last few weeks. Pregnancy can increase your risk of developing a blood clot, and unfortunately limited mobility can also increase your risk.' Cooper felt his heart thudding in his chest. He knew what he had to do next. 'You've just been unlucky, Lydia.' The words almost caught in his throat.

He watched her struggling to breathe. Her short, gasping breaths. He felt as if someone had turned back the clock two years and he was looking directly at Clara's face as she desperately tried to speak. *Don't let anything happen to our baby, Cooper.*

'You won't let anything happen to my baby, will you?'

'What?'

Lydia gasped again, clutching her oxygen mask to her face. 'You won't let anything happen to my baby, will you, Doctor?'

Cooper put his hand around hers. 'I'm going to look after you and your baby, Lydia.' From the corner of his eye he saw Melissa come back into the room, clutching the vial with the drug. He had to remain focused. It was all he could do to hold it together.

'Melissa, can you find a syringe pump, please? The streptokinase infusion needs to be administered over one hour.'

Melissa could see how unwell Lydia was. Her skin was almost translucent, her lips a tinged with blue. She was starting to understand. She was starting to appreciate how Cooper must have felt seeing his wife like this and feeling powerless to do anything to help her. It was hard enough watching Lydia, another pregnant woman, in this state. But Lydia was a stranger to her. Lydia wasn't the person she loved with all her heart and soul and carrying their child. For the first time, through her skewed pregnancy hormones, she finally, truly started to understand how he must have felt.

Cooper turned back to Lydia as the cardiac technician appeared in the room. He left Dave to go and speak to her while he explained what would be happening to his patient. 'Lydia, this woman...' he gestured at the technician '...is going to do a test called an echocardiogram. It's similar to the scans you've had to look at the baby, only this time the scan is going to look at your heart. It will help us with the diagnosis.'

Cooper moved sideways as the technician approached with the machine to take up place at the side of the bed. She started the scan within a matter of seconds, with Cooper watching the monitor on the scanner closely.

The technician spoke quietly. 'Right ventricular strain, which would agree with your diagnosis. It's probably a submassive PE.'

Cooper nodded, his head spinning. It was exactly as he had suspected. Lydia had a submassive PE, which was affecting the functioning of her heart. Patients who displayed these symptoms frequently had poorer outcomes.

His gut wrenched. This was exactly what had happened to Clara—only some of the testing equipment hadn't been available. They hadn't been able to make a definitive diagnosis and she'd been started on the preferred treatment for pregnant women—a heparin infusion. Only it had been too late and the treatment hadn't had time to work. That, and the delayed decision-making, had cost Clara her life.

Cooper took a deep breath. He could take the safe route and start Lydia on a heparin infusion. But he knew already that he wouldn't do that. Her symptoms were too severe. The clot was causing untold damage to her heart and lungs and soon it would compromise the oxygen supply to the baby. Thrombolysis was riskier. He knew that. He also knew it could break up the clot in Lydia's lungs in a matter of hours, giving her and her baby their best possible chance of survival.

He moved away from the scanner and sat down on the bed next to Lydia again. 'Lydia, the test confirms you have a blood clot in your lungs. It is affecting your breathing and how your heart is functioning. It's really important that we break the blood clot up.' He pointed at the syringe pump. 'We need to give you a medicine designed to break up the clot. We put it through a special pump...' he tapped the IV cannula in her arm

'…and it goes directly into one of your veins.' He moved his hands and laid them gently on her distended abdomen. 'We will monitor your baby the whole time the infusion is going through.'

His eyes flicked over to Melissa, who was already connecting up the electrodes to monitor the baby. 'Start the infusion,' he said. 'She'll need her blood pressure measured every five minutes for the next hour while it goes through.'

Dave gave a little nod from the top of the bed. He looked at Melissa. 'I'm going to stay in the labour ward for the next hour, Melissa, so if you need me, I'll be right here.'

Cooper gave a quick nod. 'Good. I'm going to write up Lydia's notes. I'll be back in five minutes.' He swept out the room without a backward glance.

Melissa nodded and started the infusion. She took a seat next to Lydia and reset the button on the cardiac machine to measure her blood pressure every five minutes. Melissa could feel the tears forming at the backs of her eyes. Right now Lydia's life and her baby's were hanging in the balance. She knew exactly why Dave was hanging around. If something happened, if the clot moved and Lydia went into heart failure, it was unlikely she would survive. At that point the only hope left would be to get her to Theatre and get the baby out quickly. If they didn't, the baby would die too.

Andrea appeared at the door. 'I've just got hold of your husband, Lydia. He's apparently been phoning home for the last hour, looking for you. He's on his way in.' She turned to Melissa. 'Do you need any help?'

Melissa shook her head. 'I'm going to stay in here and monitor Lydia's blood pressure.' She pointed to the second monitor at her side. 'I'm going to keep an eye on the baby too. I'll shout to you if I need anything.'

Andrea nodded, then her brow furrowed. 'What's up with Cooper?'

The question caught Melissa unawares. Other people had noticed he was struggling. Melissa shook her head. Cooper hadn't told anyone else about Clara. 'I think he had a bad experience once with a patient with a PE,' she whispered.

Andrea shrugged her shoulders and ducked

back out of the door. Melissa helped adjust Lydia's pillows to keep her in a more upright position to assist her breathing. Lydia closed her eyes and leaned back against the pillows. She was exhausted, her breathing still rapid and shallow, with no improvement yet in her colour.

Melissa sank back into her chair. The monitor sprung into life and the cuff tightened around Lydia's arm. Still hypotensive. Melissa recorded the result in the nearby chart. She wondered how soon she would see an improvement.

Her hands went automatically to her baby. Truth be told, she was glad to be sitting down. At twenty-seven weeks the shifts were getting harder and harder. But like most women due to go on maternity leave, Melissa was determined to work on as long as she could. She would hate to be sitting at home for weeks, waiting for her baby to arrive. For Melissa, it would seem like wasted time. She wanted to spend the extra time with her baby.

A few minutes later Lydia gripped her arm, her fingers digging into Melissa's wrist. She leaned forward. Melissa stood up quickly, 'What's wrong, Lydia?'

Underneath the oxygen mask Lydia's lips were tinged with blue. Melissa felt her heartbeat quicken. Lydia gasped, 'Tell Daisy that I love her.'

Melissa felt a chill descend over her body. According to Lydia's chart, Daisy was Lydia's daughter. Patients with a PE often had feelings of impending doom. It was even listed as one of the clinical signs and symptoms. She opened her mouth to say some words of comfort to Lydia but was immediately stopped by the scream from the nearby cardiac monitor as Lydia's body flopped backwards.

Immediately she pulled the emergency buzzer and started pulling the pillows from Lydia's back to lay her flat on the bed.

Within seconds the room was full of people. Dave took up position at the head of the bed. Andrea appeared at his elbow, pulling the emergency trolley behind her. She automatically handed him the laryngoscope and an endotracheal tube, which he slid into place.

Cooper appeared in the room, his face stricken. His eyes swept over the scene and stopped at the cardiac monitor. 'PEA.' Pulseless electrical activity. The type of cardiac arrest most commonly associated with PE. It meant that the heart wasn't beating properly. It was producing electrical activity without producing a pulse.

Melissa put her knee up on the bed, ensuring her hands were positioned correctly and commenced cardiac massage. Dave connected the ET tube and began bagging the patient in conjunction with Melissa's massage. His face turned to Cooper's. 'We need to take her to the emergency theatre—we've got to get this baby out.' Andrea nodded her head at his words and headed out the door. 'I'll tell the theatre staff about the imminent arrival.'

Cooper stood frozen to the spot. His eyes watching the monitor helplessly. He stared at Lydia's lifeless form as Melissa and Dave tried to breathe life into her body. The worst part of his life was being relived in front of his eyes. He'd seen this scene before. Last time he'd been shouting in the corner of the room, being held

back from Clara's body by one of the other doctors while he'd watched them perform their futile
activities. This was his worst nightmare. Another
woman was going to die in exactly the same way
that Clara had.

'Cooper?'

The voice broke into his thoughts. Melissa had
both knees up on the bed now, her face red from
the exertion of performing cardiac massage. She
was staring at him. 'Are we going to Theatre?'
she panted. Melissa's heart was thudding in her
chest. It had been years since she'd performed
cardiac massage. She'd forgotten how even the
smallest spell could make your arms and shoulders ache.

He took a deep breath. He looked downwards,
suddenly conscious of his nails digging into the
palms of his hands. He released his clenched
fists. Time was of the essence. He may have lost
his baby, but he could save this one.

'Let's go,' he said abruptly, his foot releasing
the brake at the bottom of the bed. Dave jerked
the bed suddenly towards the door, obviously forgetting Melissa was balanced on top of it. She

lurched sideways with the sudden movement and let out a scream as she landed on the floor.

'Melissa!' Cooper looked stricken at the sight of Melissa lying in a crumpled heap on the floor.

'Oh, God, Cooper, I'm sorry, I didn't realise...' Dave stood frozen to the spot.

Andrea was stuck in the doorway, trying to open the door to allow the bed to leave the room. Her voice bellowed down the corridor, 'I need another midwife in here *now*!'

Two women appeared in seconds, Andrea pointed in the direction of the bed. 'One of you on there, doing massage, the other get me a wheelchair for Melissa now!'

Cooper turned to Dave, who hadn't moved from the spot. 'Get the patient to Theatre now, Dave. I'll be there as soon as I can.'

Dave nodded silently and pulled the bed, more gently this time, towards the open doors. Andrea and Cooper helped Melissa into the wheelchair that appeared silently behind them.

'How are you, Melissa? How do you feel?'

She groaned and clutched at her stomach.

'Are you pain?'

The tears glazed over her eyes as she caught her breath. 'Cooper, I think I'm having contractions.'

Cooper's eyes met Andrea's. This was the last thing they wanted to hear. He swept the wheelchair into the room next door and lifted Melissa onto the bed. Andrea started pulling out wires from monitors, switching them on and attaching them with ruthless efficiency.

Melissa clutched Cooper's arm. 'It's too soon, Coop. I'm only twenty-seven weeks. I can't have this baby now.' The tears were flowing freely down her face as the reality of the situation swept over her.

Andrea came round and touched Cooper's arm. 'You have to go, Cooper. They need you in Theatre.'

'I can't go,' he snapped. 'There's no way I'm leaving Melissa's side. She needs me here.'

Melissa shook her head. 'You have to go, Coop. You're the only consultant here right now. Lydia doesn't stand a chance without you. And what about her baby? The surgical resident won't have a clue how to deliver a premature baby.'

Her words came out between sobs as another contraction gripped her.

Cooper shook his head frantically. 'I won't leave you, Melissa, not like this.'

Andrea tightened her grip on his arm. 'Cooper, I'll watch Melissa. I'll phone John Blair. He'll come in and oversee her care. You know you can trust him. Now, please, go.'

Cooper hesitated. John Blair was one of the most experienced obstetricians he'd ever worked with. And he did trust him.

Melissa nodded. 'Go, Cooper. Go and save Lydia and her baby.'

He looked into her green eyes. There were a hundred things he wanted to say to her right now. He didn't care that other people were in the room. Nothing mattered to him more right now than Melissa and their baby. He put his hand under her chin and bent forward. 'I'll go, Melissa, but know that there is nowhere I want to be right now other than by your side.' He leaned forward and kissed her on the mouth, wrapping his arms around her body and holding her for a few precious seconds.

'I know, Cooper,' she whispered in his ear.

And then he was gone, running down the corridor towards the theatre.

He burst through the doors and his eyes swept over the surgical registrar. 'Ever performed an embolectomy before?'

The registrar's eyes widened in shock. 'Yes, but not under these conditions.'

'Then scrub in.'

Cooper took up position at the nearby sink, pulled a sterile scrubbing brush from its container and started to scrub his hands in a frenzy. One of the theatre nurses appeared at his side, holding his gown ready. Cooper glanced at the clock. The theatre staff transferred Lydia onto the operating table and pulled the bed out of the way. One of the midwives resumed her position and continued with the massage while the theatre staff around her opened surgical packs and instruments. 'Time check?' he shouted at Dave, who was attaching Lydia to a ventilator.

Dave glanced at his watch. 'Four minutes.'

Cooper slid his arms into the green gown and held out his hands for his surgical gloves. Time was of the essence. He was usually meticulous about scrubbing for Theatre, taking at least ten minutes before putting on his surgical gloves. But this baby didn't have ten minutes.

His head was full of Melissa. Was she going to deliver? Would the contractions stop? What if he lost another baby? Another midwife appeared, pulling an incubator through the door, plugging the heat lamp above it into the nearby electrical supply. 'Paed is on his way,' she shouted. Cooper nodded. It was essential that a paediatrician was there to receive the baby after delivery. Who knew what state this baby would be in?

He took up position at the side of the bed. Beads of sweat were breaking out on his brow. 'Are you ready, Dave?'

Dave nodded. 'Cooper, I'm sorry, you know I didn't mean to...'

Cooper lifted his hand to silence him. It was trembling. His eyes fixed on his hand, willing it to stop shaking. Images of his daughter swam before his eyes. The small, blue, lifeless baby. The daughter who should have had her whole life before her. The daughter he should have taken to ballet lessons and horseriding classes. He could picture her now, a mini-version of her mother. Blonde hair in pigtails, dressed in the lilac checked dress that was the uniform of the school near where they had lived. He could see her sitting on a swing, leaning backwards, legs outstretched as the air streamed through her hair and she let out squeals of joy. He could see himself, kneeling at her bedside and reading her favourite bedtime story about caterpillars and ladybirds. All these things flitted through his mind. Then, in an instant, he was back, his hand outstretched over Lydia's prone body, the scalpel still wavering in his hand.

'Now, Cooper.' Dave's voice cut through the fog in his mind.

He took a deep breath, wiped her abdomen with Betadine and made the decisive cut. It was the quickest Caesarean section he'd ever done. One clean cut at Lydia's bikini line followed by another to free the baby from the womb. He placed both hands inside her and lifted the slippery bundle into the air. The silent baby was passed into the waiting hands of the paediatrician who had appeared at his side. He waited patiently while Cooper clipped the umbilical cord to allow him to carry the baby over to the incubator.

There was silence in the theatre. Everyone froze, afraid to move. Cooper held his breath, pain cutting through his chest. He said silent prayers over and over again. His head was thudding. He'd promised Lydia that her baby would be safe. The beads of sweat trickled freely down his brow. He shouldn't have made that promise—he'd had no right to do that.

The noise of suction pierced the theatre, followed by an angry scream from a baby. There was a collective gasp of relief. The paediatrician turned his head to the waiting spectators. 'We've got a little boy,' he said simply.

Beneath his mask, Cooper pursed his lips and let his breath out in a long, hard stream. His heart was beating frantically in his chest. He lifted his eyes from Lydia's abdomen.

Andrea appeared at the door, a mask held over her face. 'John Blair's here. He said to let you know that Melissa is still having contractions, but her waters haven't broken. The baby is showing some signs of distress but he's going to stay and monitor her. He'll let you know if you need to be there.'

Unspoken words from one professional to another. If there was going to be bad news, he would let Cooper know.

Cooper took a deep breath. More than anything in the world right now he wanted to be with Melissa. He wanted to be there, holding her hand and telling her everything would be all right. He wanted to be with the woman who made his heart sing every time he saw her. The woman who, without a doubt, was the most important thing in his life. He'd known that all along. From the second he'd seen those green eyes and they'd reminded him of his grandmother's engagement ring. His mind and body had been sending him the messages that it was time to move on. He *was* ready. But it had taken this to show him it.

He focused. He'd saved one life. It was time to try and save another. Cooper turned to the surgical registrar. 'I'm going to close now. It's up to you. Do your best, I'll assist in any way I can.'

* * *

His feet thudded down the corridor. He hadn't even changed out of his surgical scrubs or taken his mask or hat off.

He appeared at the door breathless and heart pounding. It was early evening and John Blair was sitting on the bed facing Melissa, talking to her in a low voice.

'What's wrong?' asked Cooper as he strode into the room and walked to the other side of the bed. 'What's happening?' He sat down and took Melissa's hand in his.

John pointed to the IV infusion that Melissa was connected to. 'We've had to start her on some magnesium sulphate to try and stop the contractions.' He lifted the edge of her gown. 'That was quite a blow she took when she fell, and the bruising is already beginning to show.'

Cooper drew in his breath at the livid purple bruising.

'We're lucky because her membranes haven't ruptured and after the initial jolt…' he pointed at the nearby monitor recording the foetal heart rate '…baby seems to be settling back down.'

Cooper nodded in relief. At least the baby wasn't in distress any more.

John Blair stood up and patted Melissa on the shoulder. 'I was just explaining to Melissa that she's probably worked her last shift here. If we can get these contractions stopped, I would recommend she rests easy for the rest of this pregnancy. She'll have to stay here for the next few days until we are sure everything's okay.'

Cooper nodded and stood up and reached over to shake John's hand. 'Thank you for looking after her, John. I appreciate it.'

John Blair shrugged his shoulders. 'Any time, folks.' He bent down and kissed Melissa on the cheek. 'It was my pleasure, Melissa. But just remember I'm in charge, not you.'

She nodded at him through tear-filled eyes as he left the room. Cooper resumed his position on the bed next to her and wrapped his arms around her.

'Missy, you're going to be okay.' He could see the tremor of her lips, her eyes brimming with tears.

'But it's too early, Cooper.' She was kneading her hands in her lap, over and over. 'This shouldn't be happening. What if something's wrong?' Her voice was barely a whisper.

He reached his hand towards her, curling a finger under her chin and turning her face back towards his. In the dim light of the room her green eyes seemed more electric than ever. Cooper bit his lip. It was one of the first things he'd noticed about her. It was one of the many things about her that entranced him. 'Missy—' his voice was warm and soothing '—I'm not going to let anything happen to you or the baby.' He leaned forward, wrapped both arms around her and pulled her towards him. He shifted uncomfortably as he tried to move nearer to her. 'Everything will be fine.' She was trembling and he ran his hands gently across her back and through her chestnut curls. After a few minutes the tension seemed to leave her muscles and she relaxed into him.

Her voice cut through the darkness. 'Do you promise?'

For Cooper, it took all the willpower in the world to stop his muscles stiffening in reaction to her question. He knew exactly what he had to do. No matter how difficult it was.

He drew back from their embrace and looked straight into her eyes. 'Absolutely. I promise.'

He heard her draw in a deep breath. 'How's Lydia?'

He pulled back. 'It's still touch and go. She's alive and she's been transferred to ICU at the General.' He gave a sigh as he pulled off the mask that still dangled around his neck and the theatre cap from his head. 'Her son is doing well. Apart from requiring a little oxygen and being transferred to Special Care for observation, he seems none the worse for his ordeal. At least we've got that to be thankful for.'

Melissa looked at him. For the first time since she'd known him Cooper finally looked as if he didn't have the weight of the world on his shoulders. His hair was sticking up in tufts after being trapped inside the theatre cap and his jaw and chin were shadowed with stubble. But although he looked tired, exhausted even, there was something different about him.

She shifted slightly on the bed, so he could

lean back against the pillows next to her. 'Lydia's husband wants to call the baby Cooper.'

'What?'

'He wants to name the baby after me.'

Melissa bit her lip. 'How do you feel about that?'

He ran his hands through his hair, doing little to help the ragged appearance. 'I'm not sure. We don't know what will happen with Lydia. They think that the streptokinase and the prolonged cardiac massage might have helped break up the clot. The pulmonary angiogram managed to break up the rest of the clot but we don't know how much damage had already happened.' He paused for a moment, deep in thought. 'I'm not sure if Lydia will ever wake up and get to see her baby or not.'

'But if she does, Cooper, then it's because of your actions. Your actions saved her baby's life and might well have saved her life too.'

Cooper turned to face her. 'That's all very well, but I wasn't in the place I needed to be.' His hand encircled hers. 'I wasn't with you when you needed me most and for that I'm truly sorry.'

Melissa shook her head. 'You were exactly where you needed to be. And you did exactly what you needed to do.' She gave him a little smile. 'And you look different too.'

His brow wrinkled. 'I know I must look a complete mess. But how do I look different?'

'You just do. I think today has been cathartic for you. I think you finally got to face your demons.' She raised her hand as he started to speak. 'No, don't. I think it gave me a little perspective too. I honestly didn't realise how hard this must have been for you. I know you'd told me it was hard. But today, when I saw Lydia and the state she was in, I don't know how I would have coped if that had been the woman that I loved and everything was out of my control.' She lay back against her pillows. She wasn't afraid any more. She wasn't afraid about how she felt. She didn't feel the need to hide herself from the possibility of hurt. 'I guess what I'm saying is that if you still need time, I understand. And I'm willing to give it to you because I love you. I just don't want to be your second choice.'

There. She'd said it. The words were finally out there.

His hand slid around her back. 'I don't need time, Missy.'

The words didn't sink in properly because she was trying to stop herself from crying again. She was trying her best to hold it together. 'I understand, Cooper. I understand that you wanted to keep the box with the wedding pictures and Clara's engagement ring.'

Cooper shook his head. 'No, Missy, you don't understand. I'm sorry you found that box, I meant to put it away in storage somewhere. I'll always have good and bad memories of Clara and Lily. But that's what they are now—memories. That part of my life is over.'

He pulled her close towards him, pulling a face at the IV line in her arm, which stopped him holding her just the way he wanted to.

'I haven't looked in that box in a long time. And the ring…' His eyes drifted off into the corner of the room. 'Clara knew she was going to die. She took off her engagement ring and asked me to give it to Lily. She expected me to save our baby. But I never got the chance.'

Melissa couldn't hold back tears at this point. She could see the expression on Lydia's face so clearly when she'd asked Melissa to tell her daughter that she loved her. She could only imagine that Clara had been swept by the same feeling when she'd asked Cooper to give her ring to her daughter. 'I'm so sorry, Cooper.'

'Don't be.' He pulled his arm from behind her back and knelt at the side of the bed, lifting his arms and capturing her face in his hands. 'Melissa, I realised something today that's been under my nose for months. I've already moved on. I don't need time.'

'But, Cooper—'

'Don't, Missy. You are the person that's in my dreams every night. You are the person that I think about every waking hour in every day. You are the person that makes my heart leap every time you come into a room. Today clarified everything for me. Nothing is more important to me than you and our baby.'

A single tear slid down her face again and

Cooper brushed it away with his thumb. 'Don't cry, Missy. I can't stand it when you cry—it breaks my heart. I love you and I was a fool to not tell you before this, and for that I'm sorry.'

Missy's bottom lip trembled. She was struck by the sincerity in his deep brown eyes.

'Missy, you are not my second choice—you're my only choice. How could I ever want anyone else? I love you.'

'But you don't,' she sobbed. 'You still love Clara.'

Cooper lifted his hands to brush away her tears. 'No, Missy.' He spoke quietly into her ear. 'I've loved you for some time, I just wouldn't admit that to myself.' A smile appeared on his face. 'Every time I see you it makes my heart sing. Sometimes I haven't even seen you yet, but I know that you're there. My whole body reacts whenever you're near me, and being with you makes me the luckiest man alive.'

Missy's hands trembled as she touched her stomach. 'But we don't even know what's going to happen yet.'

He placed his hands over hers. 'But whatever happens, Missy, we'll be there together. Because we're family.'

EPILOGUE

'KEEP your eyes closed,' whispered Cooper as he held his daughter in one hand and guided Melissa with the other. He stopped her right outside the door of the room she had once slept in. 'Okay, you can open it.'

Cooper held their precious bundle. Born at thirty-seven weeks and as healthy as could be. Melissa stared at the door in front of her. 'GRACE'. Carved wooden letters spelling out their daughter's name were attached to the door. She lifted her hand to touch them. Painted in shades of pink, each with a little animal carved next to it. A butterfly, a duck, a bunny, a chick and a puppy. 'It's perfect,' breathed Melissa.

Cooper pressed his palm into her back. 'Well, go on, look inside.'

Melissa pushed the door open. The room had been transformed. The stark white walls and carpet had been replaced by pale pink walls with a border of jumping bunnies and an oatmeal carpet. In the centre of the room stood a carved wooden cot, complete with pink bedding and matching mobile. Melissa gazed around in wonder as she crossed the room to touch the matching wardrobe and baby changer.

She pulled open the cupboard door. Pink dresses, pink cardigans, lilac romper suits and striped tights. And hanging up next to them was a beautiful adult-sized red wool coat. 'You remembered,' she gasped.

'Of course I remembered,' he said with a smile.

She turned her head to the window, where a leather nursing chair, complete with footrest, sat looking out over the glistening blue marina. Next to that was a white carved rocking horse with a bright red saddle.

'But when did you do this…?'

Cooper wrapped his arm around her shoulders. 'While you've been living in that luxury palace getting breakfast, lunch and dinner served to you.'

She laughed at his description of the hospital

ward where she'd spent the last few days when she'd started having contractions again. Melissa walked over to the window and fingered the pale pink curtains. 'It's just exactly like I imagined it should be,' she murmured. Her eyes fell to the window ledge, where a small parcel lay wrapped up in green paper and ribbon. 'What's this?'

Cooper had put Grace on the baby changer and was leaning over her, kissing her nose. He looked up at what she was holding in her hand. 'Oh, that's something special—unwrap it.'

Melissa gave him a little smile and sat down in the leather nursing chair, easing herself backwards so it tilted slightly and putting her feet up on the rest. She untied the thick green ribbon and pulled the paper off. Inside was a leather-bound copy of *Little Women*. Her mouth dropped open. 'You remembered? From that first night?' Her smile reached from ear to ear.

Cooper picked up the sleeping bundle and walked across the room towards her. He lowered his head, dropping a feather-light kiss on her lips. 'I've remembered everything.' A glint came into his eyes as he pointed to the red coat. 'Especially new pram, new coat. Now, what colour do you want to go for next?'

She smiled then let out a gasp as something slipped from the pages of the book. A ring. A beautiful sparkling green emerald, so big it took her breath away. 'Oh, Cooper!'

He touched her hand. 'I have to warn you that it's second-hand.' He paused while she crooked her eyebrow at him in warning. 'But this was my grandmother's ring and from the first time I saw you I thought it would be a perfect match for your eyes.'

Melissa's face broke into a slow, thoughtful smile as she looked first at the ring and then at her daughter. 'It's perfect, Cooper,' she said, 'and it's just the kind of thing I would want to pass on to my daughter.' And with that she bent forward and sealed their family with a kiss.

* * * * *

Mills & Boon® Large Print Medical

April

BREAKING HER NO-DATES RULE	Emily Forbes
WAKING UP WITH DR OFF-LIMITS	Amy Andrews
TEMPTED BY DR DAISY	Caroline Anderson
THE FIANCÉE HE CAN'T FORGET	Caroline Anderson
A COTSWOLD CHRISTMAS BRIDE	Joanna Neil
ALL SHE WANTS FOR CHRISTMAS	Annie Claydon

May

THE CHILD WHO RESCUED CHRISTMAS	Jessica Matthews
FIREFIGHTER WITH A FROZEN HEART	Dianne Drake
MISTLETOE, MIDWIFE...MIRACLE BABY	Anne Fraser
HOW TO SAVE A MARRIAGE IN A MILLION	Leonie Knight
SWALLOWBROOK'S WINTER BRIDE	Abigail Gordon
DYNAMITE DOC OR CHRISTMAS DAD?	Marion Lennox

June

NEW DOC IN TOWN	Meredith Webber
ORPHAN UNDER THE CHRISTMAS TREE	Meredith Webber
THE NIGHT BEFORE CHRISTMAS	Alison Roberts
ONCE A GOOD GIRL...	Wendy S. Marcus
SURGEON IN A WEDDING DRESS	Sue MacKay
THE BOY WHO MADE THEM LOVE AGAIN	Scarlet Wilson

Mills & Boon® Large Print Medical

July

THE BOSS SHE CAN'T RESIST	Lucy Clark
HEART SURGEON, HERO...HUSBAND?	Susan Carlisle
DR LANGLEY: PROTECTOR OR PLAYBOY?	Joanna Neil
DAREDEVIL AND DR KATE	Leah Martyn
SPRING PROPOSAL IN SWALLOWBROOK	Abigail Gordon
DOCTOR'S GUIDE TO DATING IN THE JUNGLE	Tina Beckett

August

SYDNEY HARBOUR HOSPITAL: LILY'S SCANDAL	Marion Lennox
SYDNEY HARBOUR HOSPITAL: ZOE'S BABY	Alison Roberts
GINA'S LITTLE SECRET	Jennifer Taylor
TAMING THE LONE DOC'S HEART	Lucy Clark
THE RUNAWAY NURSE	Dianne Drake
THE BABY WHO SAVED DR CYNICAL	Connie Cox

September

FALLING FOR THE SHEIKH SHE SHOULDN'T	Fiona McArthur
DR CINDERELLA'S MIDNIGHT FLING	Kate Hardy
BROUGHT TOGETHER BY BABY	Margaret McDonagh
ONE MONTH TO BECOME A MUM	Louisa George
SYDNEY HARBOUR HOSPITAL: LUCA'S BAD GIRL	Amy Andrews
THE FIREBRAND WHO UNLOCKED HIS HEART	Anne Fraser

0312 LP 2P P2 Med